Oregon READS Aloud

A Collection of 25 Children's Stories by
Oregon Authors & Illustrators

· ·

Celebrating 25 Years of SMART

Published by Graphic Arts Books

SMART
START MAKING A READER TODAY®

**GRAPHIC ARTS
BOOKS®**

S M A R T
START MAKING A READER TODAY®

**GRAPHIC ARTS
BOOKS®**

Library of Congress Control Number: 2016947864

An imprint of

Graphic Arts Books
P.O. Box 56118
Portland, OR 97238-6118
(503) 254-5591

www.graphicartsbooks.com

Printed in China

About This Book

SMART (Start Making A Reader Today)®, an Oregon-based reading nonprofit organization, is celebrating 25 years! In honor of this special milestone, we decided to publish a children's book to do what we do best: get kids excited and motivated about reading.

Over a year in the making, this project is the result of the collective creativity and commitment of people who believe in the power of books to transform children's lives. As an organization living and working in Oregon to empower our state's kids, we realized that our anniversary gave us the opportunity to showcase the rich trove of children's authors and illustrators right here in our backyard.

For a list of our contributors, please see pages 90 - 97.

In *Oregon Reads Aloud*, you'll find 25 fantastic read-aloud stories for kids, written and illustrated by members of Oregon's children's literature community. While the stories reflect a diverse range of topics, tones, and styles, they're unified by one common theme: Oregon. The book is a celebration of our state, our kids, and our families — and the power of books and reading in forming our experiences, paths, and passions. Thank you for joining us in celebrating 25 years of SMART.

We hope you enjoy *Oregon Reads Aloud!*

About SMART

For 25 years, SMART has inspired young readers in communities across Oregon by pairing trained adult volunteers to read one-on-one with PreK through third-grade children. The result: a fun, child-guided experience that builds reading skills, self-confidence, and a love of reading. Participating children also receive new books each month to keep and read with their families.

This work has been possible thanks to the tireless dedication and commitment of our volunteers, donors, educators, and supporters. In no small way, this anniversary is a celebration of the hundreds of thousands of Oregonians who've contributed their time and treasure to empowering our state's youngest readers for learning success.

We believe in an Oregon where every child can read and is empowered to succeed.

Our History

In 1991, a group of community and business leaders came together, in partnership with schools, to address the challenge that Oregon's children were routinely reading below grade level. SMART's unique, evidence-based model was developed, blending early childhood reading support, adult mentorship, and community engagement to positively impact literacy outcomes.

SMART's model works because it provides two essential ingredients children need to succeed with reading: shared one-on-one reading time and access to books.

The program launched in **1992** in **8** schools in Portland and Bend, serving **585** children.

Today, over **125,000** SMART volunteers (that's over 10,000 soccer teams!) have spent nearly **4** million hours reading one-on-one with nearly **188,000** children in **280** schools.

SMART has given these students over **2.4** million books to take home and keep. If you lined all those books up, starting at the Oregon coast, they would stretch all the way to the Idaho border.

Contents

Introduction
Sara Gets SMART

by **Jane Kirkpatrick** | illustrated by **Melissa Delzio**

First-grader Sara sat at a desk and tugged on her ear. Her mother called it her "nervous habit."

"Who's ready to start reading?" asked Mrs. Benson, the school librarian.

The older kids raised their hands. They'd been through this before. Sara pulled harder on her ear. She wanted to be ready, but she was scared. She'd heard that SMART volunteers loved to read. She hoped they could help her love to read, too.

"To read is to unveil a mystery," Mrs. Benson said.

"A mystery?" Amal asked.

"Sure. There's a mystery in every story," Mrs. Benson explained. "Will the llama find her mama? Will the princess kiss the toad? We read to find out, don't we? The author also wants us to discover the mystery inside us."

"I don't have any mystery inside me," Amal said.

"We are *all* full of mysteries, Amal. We each like different kinds of stories and that tells us something about who we are and who we might become."

Sara didn't know what Mrs. Benson was talking about, but what she said next sure caught her attention.

"Another mystery you may be wondering about is why SMART volunteers read with you."

"Because they like us!" said Maryanne.

"Yes, they *do* like you," Mrs. Benson said. "But they also know reading helps you see new worlds and new ways to be in this world."

Madison raised her hand next. "I always feel better after reading with my volunteer. She makes me laugh and then I try harder to read the words I don't know. She helps me. She says she'll never stop reading and neither will I."

Mrs. Benson smiled. "That's what SMART is all about: helping kids read and get excited about books. Soon, we'll discover the mysteries inside the books and inside ourselves." She pulled out a piece of paper. "Now, it's time to meet our volunteers."

Sara's heart beat a little faster as Mrs. Benson read names off the list. Finally, it was her turn. "Sara, come meet Mr. Ortiz."

A large man with a beard like Santa Claus stepped forward and shook her hand. "Hello, Sara," he said. "Are you ready to pick out a book?"

She picked up a book. "*Beatrice's Goat*," Mr. Ortiz said, grinning. "Great choice!"

"You've read it before?" Sara was surprised.

"Many times," said Mr. Ortiz. "When my daughter was young, it was her favorite. I bet you and I can read this story together. Would you like to try?"

Sara nodded. She did want to try.

All around she could hear the quiet voices of children and grown-ups starting to read their stories. Slowly, Sara began page one, "If you . . . were . . . to visit . . ."

She sounded out each word, and Mr. Ortiz helped her when she couldn't make out the letters. Together they looked for the mystery inside the story. And Sara hoped to discover — through reading — the mystery inside herself.

Jane Kirkpatrick is the author of over 25 books and historical novels. She lives in Central Oregon and is a great friend to SMART. ■

Go, Bikes, Go!

written & illustrated by **Addie Boswell**

Big bikes
Small bikes
Extra tall bikes

Old bikes
New bikes
Built-for-two bikes

Bikes with three wheels
Bikes with four
Doesn't that bike
need one more?

Bikes on mud slicks
Bikes on snow
Bikes on sand dunes
Go, bikes, go!

Bikes do wheelies
Bikes do jumps
Yikes! Those bikes hit
lots of bumps!

Bikes can push things
Bikes can pull
Uh-oh, flat tire —
Roll, bikes, roll . . .

Bikes play polo
Bikes play chase
Bikes zoom downhill
Race, bikes, race!

Bike brakes squeeeeeel
Bike horns BLOW
Bikes get jumbled
Whoa, bikes, whoa!

Bikes tow families
Bikes tow trees
Dogs tow bikes and
bikes tow skis

Bikes spray water
Bikes shoot fire
Bikes dance high on
tightrope wire!

Bikes wear feathers
Bikes wear shoes
Who rides bikes
inside of zoos?

Can bikes swim?
Can bikes fly?
Which bikes would
you like to try? ■

Will and the Piper

by **Kim T. Griswell** | illustrated by **Lisa Mundorff**

Will wasn't born great. How could he be? He had 22 mouse brothers and 16 mouse sisters, all of whom were bigger or faster or braver or stronger than he was.

"The only thing Will is good at is hiding," his siblings teased.

Will lived in the perfect place for hiding: the Elizabethan Theatre in the tiny town of Ashland, Oregon. The theater was round and its roof open. Rows of green seats arced up from the diamond-shaped stage. A Tudor-style stage house stood at the back. With four stage levels, a musician's gallery[1], and a moat[2], the theater had plenty of hiding places.

Each afternoon the mice played hide-and-seek. To Will's siblings, it was just a game. But to him it was more. "I want to be the best hider in history," he declared.

"Why?" asked his brother Falstaff.

"Because we mice must never be seen," Will answered.

"If you're seen," their mother cautioned, "Stage Manager will call the Piper."

The Piper. The name made Will's fur stand on end.

Legend said when the Piper played his penny whistle, mice couldn't resist. They were drawn to his music and the Piper scooped them into his gunnysack. Once caught, he drove them far away and they never saw home again.

1. musician's gallery: a loft where musicians play.
2. moat: a shallow ditch that surrounds the main stage.

One afternoon, Will hid in his favorite spot: squeezed behind the leg of seat BB101. From there, he had a clear shot to Home Base, plus he could see most of the theater. He spotted Juliet skittering down the vomitorium[3], Hamlet hiding in the musician's gallery, and Hecate creeping along the moat.

Will watched and waited, but soon the warm sun lulled him to sleep. He woke with a start when the seat squeaked above him. He noticed a black velvet sky above the theater. Glowing lights illuminated the stage. A trumpet sounded and the audience hushed.

"Oh no!" Will cried, when a man stepped out of the shadows stage left. In his hand he held a shiny brass penny whistle.

Will froze. "The Piper!"

3. vomitorium: a ramp leading to the lower levels of the theater.

13

The Piper placed the whistle to his lips. Music trilled out, swift and sweet, like a creek gathering speed as it cascades down a mountain. Will swayed toward it then shook himself. He was hidden. All he had to do was stay put. But the music flowed faster and faster . . . its pull grew stronger and stronger . . . until . . .

"Mouse!" screeched a girl in the front row.

"Mouse!" roared a man from the balcony.

Will couldn't believe his eyes.

His brothers and sisters streamed toward the stage. By ones and by twos and by threes[4], they wove toward the Piper, as if caught in a midsummer night's dream.

"Mother!" cried Will. But it was too late. She flitted right up to the Piper and sat at his feet. The Piper plucked each of them up and stuffed them into his gunnysack.

Will's knees trembled. "What good was being the greatest hider in history," he thought, "if the Piper captures my family?"

"I can't stay hidden!" he decided. "But how can I defeat the Piper's song?"

Will noticed some spilled popcorn. That would work! He stuffed a piece in each ear and bolted toward the stage.

The Piper spotted Will. His fingers ran up and down the whistle. But Will kept coming. The Piper's cheeks turned red and his eyes bulged out. But Will didn't stop. He raced onto the stage and straight up the Piper's leg. He scrambled up his chest and onto his shoulder, then launched himself out onto the penny whistle.

4. from Shakespeare's tragic play *Coriolanus*.

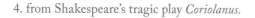

The Piper squealed and tossed the penny whistle high into the air. It rose over the audience, spinning toward the black velvet sky. Will clung to the whistle's holes. Down below, he saw the Piper drop his gunnysack. He saw his family spill out and race for the safety of the wings.

Down, down, down the whistle fell, landing with a CRASH!

Will woke to a throbbing head and a cacophony of mouse voices. For a moment he had no idea where he was. Then he remembered. "The Piper!" He sat up so quickly he saw stars.

"Lie still." His mother eased him back down. "You're home safe, son."

"We're all safe," said Juliet. "Thanks to you!"

Will's mother gave his paw a squeeze. "Some are born great. Some achieve greatness. But you, my dear Will, have had greatness thrust upon you[5]. And you saved us all." ■

5. from Shakespeare's comic play *Twelfth Night*, *or What You Will*.

First Day Jitters

by **Dawn Babb Prochovnic** | illustrated by **Abigail Marble**

First day jitters. Wide awake.
Topsy, turvy tummy ache.

Lumpy oatmeal. Eat it slow.
Need to hurry. Time to go.

Rainy sidewalk. Wave good-bye.
Noisy bus ride. Feeling shy.

Giant hallway. Crowded room.
Heart ker-thumping. **Boom, boom, boom.**

Find my classroom. Spot my hook.
Meet my teacher, Mrs. Cook.

Draw a picture. Write my name.
Play a get-to-know-you game.

Cut some paper. Squeeze the glue.
Color in the gold and blue.

Choose a geode from the box.
Learn that thundereggs are rocks.

Dig for treasures in the sand.
Hold a fossil in my hand.

Paint a landmark. Crater Lake.
Oops, I made a big mistake.

Messy fingers, **drip, drip, drip.**
Soggy sneakers, **slip, slip, slip.**

Sticky bandage. Salty tear.
Wish my friends from home were here.

Fun!

Pet the hamster. Water plants.
Feed the salmon. Watch the ants.

Belly rumbles. Time for lunch.
Sandwich, carrots, fruity punch.

Put the compost in the bin.
Wipe the jelly off my chin.

Join the line to go outside.
Climb the rock wall. Brave the slide.

Twirl a jump rope. Spin and drop.
Skip and gallop. **Hop, hop, hop.**

Laugh and giggle with new friends.
Hold a hand when recess ends.

Quiet voices. Carpet time.
Read a story. Chant a rhyme.

Learn the signs for smart and fun.
Practice spelling *Oregon*.

Count the pennies. Stack the blocks.
Set the hands on tiny clocks.

Time for clean up. Choose a chore.
Coats and backpacks out the door.

Find my school bus. Step right on.
First day jitters, *gone, gone, gone.* ■

Have Spacesuit, Will Travel

by **Curtis C. Chen** | illustrated by **Natalie Metzger**

It was a bright and sunny morning, like it always was in low Earth orbit. Angel stepped out of the airlock and onto the surface of her home: the disk-shaped space station *Multnomah*. She wore an old-fashioned jet-suit and carried a very important package.

"I'll get you there," Angel said to the small metal case attached to her belt.

"Who are you talking to?" said her little sister Carolyn over the radio.

"Nobody," Angel replied. "Any sign of trouble?"

"You mean besides you?"

"I mean on the scanners. Is there anybody out here?"

The jet-suit, which Angel had rescued from her family's storage bay, had a rocket backpack with three thrusters and full manual controls! Nobody made self-propelled spacesuits like this anymore.

Unfortunately, that also meant the jet-suit's computer was too old to scan for space traffic. So Angel needed Carolyn to scan the area and warn her about any other spacewalkers nearby. Angel didn't want to run into anyone while she was sneaking around.

"Coast is clear," Carolyn said.

"Moving out now." Angel nudged the suit's throttle control forward. The jets were more powerful than she expected, and she nearly crashed into the station.

"Use short bursts!" Carolyn said. "Accelerate *slowly.*"

"Don't tell me how to fly!" Angel said. "I know how to fly."

"You know how to play video games. There's a difference."

"Just give me a map reading, okay?"

The jet-suit controls felt different out here than in the gymnasium where Angel had practiced, sneaking in after school every day for the past month. It took her a few minutes to get the hang of balancing all three thrusters to move in a straight line.

Soon, she was speeding toward the station's spaceport.

"You're almost there," Carolyn said. "Another 50 meters, then turn 45 degrees up."

"It's *positive pitch, four-five degrees*," Angel corrected. "You say the numbers separately."

"Why do I need to learn made-up words when I can just say 'turn'?" Carolyn asked. "And I know how to count, thank you very much."

"It's how pilots talk. I'll explain later," Angel said. "*Pitching up* now."

She pulled the control stick back with her thumb. The spaceport's cargo docks came into view.

"Okay, I'm lined up." Angel felt nervous as she looked over the jagged mess of the cargo docks. Maneuvering around them would be tricky. "Where's the ship?"

"Straight ahead of you. Bay 95. All the way at the end."

Before Angel could ask which end, an alarm sounded and red lights flashed inside her helmet.

"What's that noise?" Carolyn shouted.

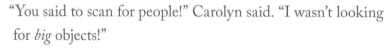

Angel spun around. An enormous space freighter was coming in to dock with *Multnomah*. And Angel was floating directly between it and the station!

"Incoming spaceship!" Angel said. "Why didn't you warn me?"

"You said to scan for people!" Carolyn said. "I wasn't looking for *big* objects!"

Angel felt unusually calm as she pressed both of her suit's palm controls.

Carolyn was right: it wasn't like a video game. Angel felt the backpack jets push against her body. Three thrusters worked together to shove her away from the freighter.

When she was safely out of the way, Angel's hands started shaking. Her stomach fluttered. More alerts flashed in her helmet display, warning that she had exceeded speed limits and entered a restricted area. But all Angel heard was the blood rushing past her ears — until her mother's voice came on the radio.

"Angel Daria Chace!" Mom did not sound happy. "What are you doing out there?"

Angel touched the metal case on her belt. It had been a week since the funeral in Hermiston. "I'm helping Grandma," she answered.

She angled back toward her target, a robotic waste disposal ship. The jet-suit was pretty easy to steer now that she knew how the controls felt.

"What do you mean?" Mom paused. "Angel! Did you take your grandmother's ashes?"

"She wanted to be buried in space." Angel slowed down, then slapped the magnetic case containing her grandmother's ashes onto the side of the disposal ship. "I'm sending her into the Sun."

"Angel, you get back here right now!"

The radio buzzed, and a new voice filled Angel's helmet. "Unidentified pilot, this is *Multnomah* Traffic Control. Please leave the restricted area and meet authorities at airlock three-nine."

A wide grin spread across Angel's face. No one had ever called her a *pilot* before.

"The captain of the freighter that almost pancaked you says he 'wants to meet the cowboy who can dance like that in an antique rocket suit.'"

"Yee-haw!" Angel hollered. Then she remembered her radio channel was open. "I mean, sir, yes, sir!" ■

Where Is My Mami?

by **Carmen T. Bernier-Grand** | illustrated by **Robin Kerr**

Inside the Gresham *correo*, Mami stops to write something on the box she's mailing to my Eugene cousins. I stand right behind her to make sure she doesn't get lost like she did yesterday at the *biblioteca*. A *señora* comes in with a tall ladder of boxes. I walk around her. How can she see behind so many *paquetes*?

The line is now as long as a *serpiente*. I stand in front of a *señor* and look up at his black *bigote*. That mustache looks like a flying *pájaro*.

¡Ay! Where is my mami?

Is she still writing? Is she behind the *señora* with the tall ladder of *paquetes*? Is she in front of the *señor* with the black *pájaro bigote*?

"Ana María!" I hear her panic.
"Mami, please," I tell her, *"stay by me!"*
My mami gets scared when she can't find me.

At La Tapatía Mercado, I help my mami push the *carrito*. I throw in a bunch of *plátanos*. I take three bites from a *manzana*.

English Translations

Correo: Post office	**Señor:** Adult man	**Manzana:** Apple
Biblioteca: Library	**Bigote:** Mustache	**Masa:** Corn-based dough
Señora: Adult woman	**Pájaro:** Bird	**Chaquetas:** Jackets
Paquetes: Packages	**Carrito:** Cart	**Juguetes:** Toys
Serpiente: Snake	**Plátanos:** Bananas	

¡Ay! Where is my mami?

Is she by the cilantro that is taking a shower? Is she getting *masa* to make tamales?
Is she buying me one those piñatas?

"Mami?" I call. And then I find her. "Mami, stay by me!" I tell her again,
"So you don't get lost."

The mall is big and noisy. So much to see! Under a rack of Mexican *chaquetas,*
I spot Mami's red flip-flops. *¡Ay, no!* They are not my mami's!

¡Ay! Where is my mami?

Is she trying on dresses? Is she looking for purses?
Is she buying me *juguetes?*

Where is my mami?

Oh no, my mami is lost! "Mami!" I call. "Mamiiii!"

"Ana María!" Mami hugs me. "That was scary," she says.

"Yes, it was," I tell her.

This time I hold my mami's hand. That way I stay
with my mami, and my mami stays by me,
so she doesn't get lost again. ■

Dear Bigfoot

by **Robin Herrera** | illustrated by **Katy Towell**

DEAR BIGFOOT,

My mom says I have to write you a thank-you letter after what you did last week, even though I already thanked you and everything, but oh well. I bet you have a mom who makes you write thank-you letters when people (or Bigfeets) do something nice for you.

So here is my thank-you letter.

Thanks, Bigfoot!

Sincerely,
Jade Brownstein

DEAR BIGFOOT (AGAIN),

Mom says the last letter I wrote barely counts as a thank-you letter. I asked her what a thank-you letter was supposed to have in it, anyway. She says a "sincere" thank-you should do.

Thank you so much, Bigfoot! I sincerely thank you a bunch for saving us from the mean bear in Wolf Creek.

Sincerely (again),
Jade Brownstein

DEAR BIGFOOT!

Guess who. Mom says just adding "sincere" to stuff doesn't make it sincere. So I baked you some cookies too. After the bear ran away you mentioned that you liked chocolate chip cookies.

Nothing says sincerity like baking!
(That's what Grandma always says.)

Anyway, you're probably busy with your book group. Maybe you can share these with the other Bigfeets. Also I have a suggestion for your club: we read a book called *My Side of the Mountain* in class. I didn't like it but I think you would because you like the outdoors and camping and stuff.

All the best,
(Mom told me to stop writing "Sincerely")
Jade Brownstein

HI BIGFOOT,

Mom thinks my last letter wasn't thankful enough. Maybe because I didn't say "Thank you" in it, which I had forgotten. I was too busy being sincere! I am really glad that you scared that bear away from our tent because we could have been hurt if you hadn't. And I'm glad that you shared your tea with us after we found out the bear ate all our food. So thank you!!!

If you see that bear, tell it that I am NOT thankful to it at all.

Warm wishes,
Jade Brownstein

DEAR BIGFOOT,

Mom said my last letter was just fine! But I wanted to write you again anyway and invite you to my birthday party. I'm turning 10 next month and I told Mom I wanted to have a barbecue. I don't know if you know what that is, but I bet you'd like it a lot!

You don't have to bring me a present. I guess if you really want to you can bring me a pinecone maybe. I learned how to make bird feeders at school, so if you get me a really big pinecone I can make one big enough for all the birds in my backyard.

Hope to see you soon,
(Grandma says that's a good letter-ender)
Jade Brownstein

DEAR BIGFOOT,

I wanted to show you my bird feeder so I'm putting a picture in with this letter. I hope you had fun at the party! I know you were worried about other people seeing you. I should have told you that you were the only one I invited.

The pinecone was perfect! And so big! I didn't know they could get that big. Even Grandma was surprised. *Not as surprised as when you started dancing with her, though.* Anyway, I think I want to try building another bird feeder. This one just gets blue jays and sparrows. They're okay to look at, but I know there are hummingbirds out there too. Mom

says maybe for my next birthday we could come visit you and I could see some of the birds that live in the forest.

As long as there aren't any bears around.

Your friend,
Jade Brownstein

DEAR BIGFOOT,

THANK YOU for coming to my party. Mom was mad that I didn't put that in my last letter.

And thank you for being my friend. Mom didn't tell me to say that, but I wanted to anyway.

Love,
Jade Brownstein

P.S. That picture I took of you at the party came out all blurry! You'll have to send me a good one to put on my wall. ■

Kira's Imagineering

by **Sonja Thomas** | illustrated by **Elizabeth Goss**

As the autumn sun inched toward the horizon, Kira the Swift flew round and round and round the Chapman Elementary smokestack with her family of 5,000. Just like last night. And the night before that. A never-ending spin cycle — swirling, whirling, up and down — the dark brown birds circled the tall brick chimney, getting ready to roost in the chimney for the night.

Down below, hundreds of humans sat on the school lawn, whistling and cheering. Kira didn't understand what all the fuss was about.

Kira veered away from the flock and landed on the side of her favorite tree, her claws gripping the bark. She closed her eyes.

A squirrel scuttled down the tree trunk and sat beside her. "What are you doing?" he asked.

"I'm *imagineering*," Kira answered, opening one eye.

"What's that?" The squirrel yanked an acorn off the branch.

"It's a way I can be something new. I just close my eyes and imagine: What if I was an emperor penguin? I'd have tuxedo feathers and flippers instead of wings. I'd be as tall as a human child, not tiny like a crayon."

"What else do you imagine?" the squirrel asked.

"I imagine myself as an ostrich, my neck and legs stretched long," Kira said. "I'm the fastest two-legged animal in the world!"

"My turn!" said the squirrel. "I imagine myself as a parrot, sailing the Caribbean Sea perched on a pirate's shoulder. My days are filled with swashbuckling adventure, treasure hunting for — "

"Acorns!" Kira finished. Kira and the squirrel laughed.

Suddenly, a shadow swooped overhead. Squeaks and chirps cut through the air. The crowd down below gasped.

"A hawk!" the squirrel shrieked. His half-eaten nut plunked to the ground as he disappeared.

The swifts skittered and scattered, chattering in fright. They zigged and zagged. They cut to the left. They veered to the right. Kira watched her family trying to escape, but the hawk stayed right on their tails.

Kira trembled. If only she really had long ostrich legs or was as tall as an emperor penguin or had a mighty pirate sword. Then she could save her family. But she wasn't an ostrich or a penguin. She wasn't even a parrot!

"Wait . . ." she thought. "Maybe I can *imagineer* a way to beat that hawk!"

Kira imagined no more swarm. No more skitter, no more scatter. She imagined something big and strong — a bird supersized enough to chase off the hawk.

That's it!

Kira bolted into the air.

"We may be tiny," Kira shouted, "but we are 5,000 strong! We more than outnumber that old hawk."

Kira shared her plan. Her family followed her lead. Crescent-shaped wings aflutter, their skedaddle spun into a twister — *Zip!* *Zoom!* — they picked up speed and . . .

The crowd of humans gasped as a giant bird took shape. Then the giant bird turned and began chasing the hawk.

With a loop-dee-loop the hawk switched direction, flapping faster and faster away from the cyclone of swifts on his tail. The swifts drove him higher and higher until the flock stretched as tall as a skyscraper. The hawk's wings thrashed harder, as he tried to escape. Then with one last flap, he disappeared over the horizon and was gone.

The humans below clapped and cheered, *"Hip, hip, hooray!"*

The swifts buzzed in celebration. "Kira saved the day!" they chanted.

The flock, now safe, returned to their "Swiftnado" dance, swirling and whirling around the brick chimney. As the harvest moon rose, the dark mass of birds funneled into the flue. Each swift took a turn, plunging in tail first. Tucked inside, feet clinging to the wall, their bodies overlapped one another to keep warm.

Kira snuggled in with her family feeling happy, and imagined the excitement the next day would bring.

Author's Note

Vaux's swifts (pronounced "voxes" like "foxes") migrate south every fall to Central America and Venezuela. With tree hollows scarce, swifts often nest in brick chimneys. Each September, Portland's Chapman Elementary School chimney hosts the largest known roost of migrating swifts, with estimates of up to 15,000 birds! ∎

Meshmesh on Wheels

by **Cathy Camper** | illustrated by **Linda Dalal Sawaya**

Kalil and Aqila were skateboarding maniacs. They skated at the playground every day after school, banging their boards against the pavement — *click, click, clack* — and yelling out silly names for their moves.

"Hop the Willamette!" *Fwooot* — Kalil jumped a puddle.

"Mount Rainier — *bump* — Mount Adams — *thump* — Mount St. Helens — *clump* — and Mount Hood!" Aqila shouted, hopping up the stairs.

"Walla Walla Onion Rings!" they both cried, skating circles round and round. *Swoosh whoosh, swoosh whoosh.*

Uncle and Auntie lived next door to the playground. They enjoyed eating hummus and tortillas on their porch in peace. *They didn't like the noise.*

"You tell those kids to go away!" Auntie said.

"You tell those kids to be quiet!" Uncle replied. But they were both too old for yelling.

"What we need is a dog. A dog would scare those kids away," Uncle said.

Uncle and Auntie went to the animal shelter. They looked at big dogs, little dogs, wiener dogs and dogs with ears like pancakes. Finally, they spotted a bulldog. She stared sadly at them from her cage, her jowly chin on her paws.

"We'll take her!" Uncle told the volunteer. "Bulldogs are rough and tough."

The volunteer tried to warn them. "She's not rough, she's sad. She's not tough, she's gloomy. And she never barks."

But Uncle and Auntie wouldn't listen. They paid for the bulldog and brought her home. Every day after school, they put the bulldog out on their porch.

"Bark at those kids," they told her. "Chase those noisy skateboarders away!" they demanded.

But the bulldog just flopped down and sighed. "What's wrong with this dog?" Uncle asked.

"Maybe she needs more love," Auntie replied.

So they bought her a soft bed, a giant bone and a purple squeaky toy. The bulldog thanked them with wet kisses. But when they put her out on the porch, she lay her wrinkly chin on her paws and moped.

One day when Kalil and Aqila tumbled out of their house and headed for the playground, they noticed something new.

"What's that?" Aqila asked, pointing to the lump on the porch.

"A bulldog!" Kalil replied. "What's your name, doggie?" The dog sniffed Kalil's hand. *"Oooh, your face is wrinkly like a dried-up apricot!"*

"Let's call her Meshmesh," Aqila said. "Apricot in Arabic!"

"Come on, Meshmesh! Come skate with us!" Kalil threw down his board, aimed at the playground.

Kalil pushed off. "Yallah*, Meshmesh!"

To their surprise, the dog's eyes lit up. Meshmesh hopped off her bed and trotted down the steps.

*Yallah means "Come on, let's go" in Arabic.

31

"Yallah, yallah!" the kids shouted, skating toward the playground, Meshmesh trotting at their heels.

"Jump the Willamette!" Kalil yelled, showing off for the dog. He made it over the puddle, but landed on the pavement instead of his board. The skateboard rolled away and stopped in front of the dog.

Meshmesh sniffed the board. She put up her left front paw. Her left back paw followed. With her right legs, she started pushing.

The skateboard was rolling. Meshmesh jumped on board!

"A dog that can skate!?!" Kalil stared in amazement. Slowly, Meshmesh rolled across the playground. Whenever the board slowed, she pushed again. Her eyes were shining. She sniffed the air. She yelped with joy.

"The Bulldog Glide," Kalil named her moves.

"What's all that noise?" Uncle asked, peering down from the porch.

"Who's doing all that barking?" Auntie complained, setting down her tortilla and hummus.

"Uncle, Auntie, look! Your dog Meshmesh can skate!" Aqila said.

While everyone watched, Meshmesh glided gracefully up to the porch. She hopped off the skateboard and raced up the steps. Before Uncle knew it, Meshmesh leaped up, grabbed the tortilla right out of his hand and gobbled it up.

"Well, well," Uncle shook his head.

"A Meshmesh who skates," Auntie replied, patting the satisfied dog on her head.

"We have an old board she can use," the kids suggested. Meshmesh lay down on her bed and snored.

"I guess we can handle a little noise," Auntie said. And she passed the kids some hummus and tortillas.

Author's Note

Meshmesh is based on a real Portland bulldog I once saw gliding across a parking lot. When she reached the end, she waited for her owner to turn the board around, then she hopped on and glided back. "How did you teach her to do that?" I asked. "I didn't," her owner replied. "When I got her from the pound she just moped all day. Then my nephew came by with his skateboard and she perked up, hopped on, and that was that." ■

The Legend of the Mountains' Quarrel

by **Damien & Heléna Macalino** | illustrated by **Doug Roy**

Long before mankind cast fishing nets into the great river Columbia and carved ancient pictures into the towering cliffs of the Gorge, Hood sat beside the river and gazed happily at his boulder of golden glowing sunstone.

Beside him, his sister Helen talked to her petrified wood as if it were a dear friend, "How beautiful you are! As smooth as the beaver's pelt, as purple as the iris, and as round as a fresh, plump blueberry."

But Hood knew his sunstone was far more beautiful than Helen's plain petrified wood. "Let's play Boulder on the Bridge," he said to interrupt her annoying song of admiration.

"I'd be delighted!" Helen said. She ran across the Bridge of the Gods, the rough red archway that spanned the river. Hood watched in irritation as chunks of stone tumbled into the water with each of the giantess's footfalls.

"Watch your step! That's our only way across!" he growled.

Hood climbed to the grassy meadow at his end of the bridge to start the game. From here, he could see the glade at the center of the bridge where he needed to throw his boulder to win.

"Ready, set, throw!" Helen shouted.

Hood threw his sunstone boulder as hard as a raging grizzly bear. Helen threw her giant piece of petrified wood as precise as a hawk's strike. Hood's sunstone collided with Helen's petrified wood and hit the bridge.

BOOM! Her cherished rock exploded in a purple storm.

The brother and sister gasped.

"How could you do this?!" Helen cried.

But then they heard a thundering rumble. CRACK!

The bridge was collapsing!

After a few moments of falling rocks, they stared in shock at the empty space where the bridge used to be.

"There's no way to get across now," Hood realized. They would no longer be able to play Boulder on the Bridge; they would no longer be able to sit together and admire their stones.

But the worst part was that he had broken Helen's glorious petrified wood . . . and her heart. It was all his fault. He had gotten mad and thrown his stone too hard. What had he done?!

Hood shouted to Helen, "I promise to find every single piece of your stone. And when I do, I promise to bring it to you, no matter what."

Helen turned away and disappeared into the forest. His heart heavy, Hood started his search.

Weeks, months, and years passed by without any sign of another way across the wide, wide river. Hood's pile of petrified wood grew and grew. Once, he thought he caught a glimpse of his sister across the river, her head hanging low . . . but it was only a tree swaying in the wind. ***Oh, how he missed her!***

Finally, the day came when Hood had collected all of the petrified wood. Piece by piece he reassembled Helen's boulder. As the rock came back to life, Hood carried it to the edge of the shore and called to the beavers, ducks, otters, and fishes.

"Would you swim this petrified wood to my sister, Helen, on the other side of the river?"

The animals gathered together and Hood placed the boulder on their backs.

As the animals swam across the great Columbia, Hood called to his sister. "Helen, I kept my word. I brought your stone back to you."

Helen emerged from the trees and peered down at her revived petrified wood. But her face did not light up. She walked down to the river and picked up the boulder.

"Thank you, Hood, but seeing this stone made me realize something: Yes, I am happy to have my rock back, but it's more important to be back with you."

Hood's eyes filled with tears. "I feel the same, sister. But how can we be together again?"

"What's your most favorite thing of all — other than me?" Helen asked.

"My sunstone." Hood understood what Helen was saying. He knew the one way they would never again be hidden from each other's sight.

The brother and sister lifted their stones high into the air. A blinding, white flash of light filled the Gorge. On the southern horizon and the northern horizon, two mountains appeared that day. And now, Mount Saint Helens and Mount Hood can admire their stones together for eternity.

Authors' Note

While this is an original story, at your library you can find many beautiful Native American legends about the two mountains. As for their beloved boulders, Helen's petrified wood is the state stone of Washington and Hood's sunstone is Oregon's! ■

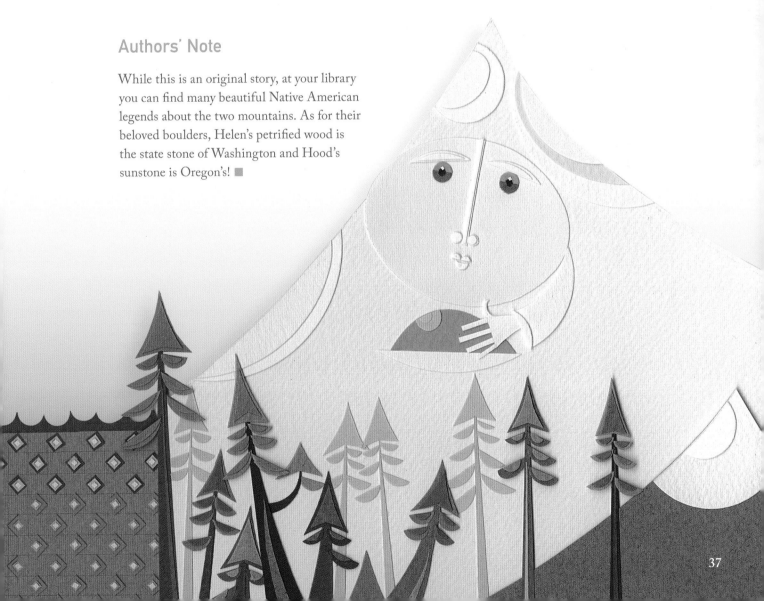

Raccoon's Tooth

written & illustrated by **Nancy Coffelt**

Raccoon watched the dandelion puff float away on the wind.

"Don't forget to make a wish," said Grandfather.

Raccoon made a wish and then — felt a wiggle. "My tooth is loose! What will I do with it when it falls out?"

"You could give it to the ground," said Grandfather. "Then it would join all the shiny pebbles there."

"What if Mole rolls it away? No," said Raccoon. *"I'll keep my tooth."*

The sun rose higher than the mountains and Raccoon's tooth wiggled even more. "Grandfather, what will I do with my tooth if it falls out?"

"You could give it to the lake. Then it would join all the shiny whitecaps there."

"What if Trout gobbles it up? No," said Raccoon. *"I'll keep my tooth."*

The sun sank low and Raccoon and Grandfather sat under their tree. Raccoon pushed at her tooth with her tongue. "Grandfather, what will I do with my tooth if it falls out?"

"You could give it to the sky," said Grandfather. "Then it would join all the shiny stars there."

"What if Bat snatches it out of the air?" Raccoon shook her head.

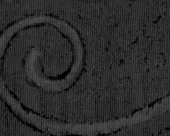
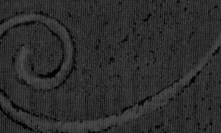

Late that night a great storm rose. The wind raged and Raccoon and Grandfather's great fir tree swayed back and forth.

"Grandfather!" Raccoon called. "My tooth fell out!" A great gust shook the tree. "And now I know what to do."

Raccoon scampered to the end of the branch and hurled her tooth into the storm. "What are you doing?" asked Grandfather.

"I gave my tooth to the wind!" said Raccoon. "Now it will be with all the wishes — including mine."

"What was your wish?" asked Grandfather.

"That you'd stay with me forever."

"Well," said Grandfather. "I have given a tooth to the ground, so whenever you see the shiny pebbles, I'll be there. And I have given a tooth to the lake, so whenever you see the whitecaps, I'll be there. And I have given a tooth to the sky, so whenever you count the stars, I'll be there, too."

"Then it was a good wish," said Raccoon.

"A very good wish," agreed Grandfather.

With that settled, they snuggled back in the fir boughs and let the wind rock them to sleep. ■

The Camp Cook

by **Susan Blackaby** | illustrated by **David Hohn**

Adapted from a retelling by S.E. Schlosser

When my great-granddad, Hap, was just a kid, he saw a "Help Wanted" ad in the *Baker City* weekly.

Hap hiked up to the logging camp to see about the job. When he got there, he couldn't believe his eyes. Hap knew that Paul Bunyan was the biggest lumberjack ever to swing an ax. But Paul Bunyan was tall. Paul Bunyan was very tall. He was as tall as a Sitka spruce! His blue ox, Babe, was larger than a locomotive!

"Hello, son." Paul Bunyan's booming voice made the ground shake. "What brings you to this part of the range?"

Hap's ears rang and his head clanged and his teeth rattled. "I'm here about the job, sir," he said.

Paul Bunyan put his hands on his hips and stared down at Hap. "Have you got any talents?"

"I don't think so," said Hap.

Paul frowned. "Do you know any tricks?"

"Not really," said Hap.

Paul tapped his chin. "Have you got any skills at all?"

"Nope," said Hap.

Paul Bunyan scratched his head. Then he shrugged. "In that case, I guess you're hired!"

Hap grinned. "Thank you, sir," he said. "What do you want me to do?"

Paul's belly growled like a grumpy grizzly bear. Babe snorted.

"Well, son, I am feeling a mite peckish. And Babe here is downright hungry. How about some pancakes? Whip up a batch for me and the crew. If you do a good job, you can be the new cook."

Hap nodded. "Okay!"

Hap had cooked pancakes plenty of times, but right away he saw that this was going to be a different kettle of fish. For one thing, the griddle was the size of a schoolroom! Hap loaded the stove with firewood until it glowed like a volcano.

Then he cracked a mountain of eggs into a dish the size of a swimming pool. He added a truck full of flour and a dozen washtubs of milk.

To get everything ready, Hap needed some help. "Listen up, troops!" Hap called. "You'll get extra pancakes if you help me out!"

Hap soon had lots of helpers, and they all got to work. A dozen loggers each grabbed an oar and started stirring the batter. Six more slid across the griddle on sleds made of bacon so the pancakes wouldn't stick. Six more helped Hap dump buckets of batter onto the griddle. The batter spattered and sizzled, bubbled and puffed. Hap and the crew cooked up a stack of pancakes two stories tall.

Would it be enough? Maybe not!

The table was 10 miles long!

Hap loaded pancakes onto platters as big as river rafts. Servers steered pony carts up and down the table to deliver supplies. Paul Bunyan ate 50 helpings. Babe ate 65 helpings and licked all the plates clean.

Hap was proud, but he was as worn out as a wagon wheel on the Oregon Trail by the time he was done. Every part of him ached from head to toe. He hobbled to a seat and plopped down.

"Congratulations, Hap, you've got yourself a job." Paul wiped his mouth on the bedsheet he used for a napkin. "That short stack should keep me going for a spell. Babe and I will be back for supper at six sharp." ■

Lionel and Pip
One tinkers. One studies. Best ever buddies.

by **Stephanie Shaw** | illustrated by **Susan Boase**

Lionel was a doer. Pip was a thinker. Usually they made a great team.

One morning Lionel decided to do something adventurous.

"I'm going to find the dairy," declared Lionel. "And get us some cheese!"

"Great!" said Pip. "I'll draw up a map and make a list of supplies."

"I don't need all that stuff! I'm a *field* mouse!" Lionel declared. "And you'll just slow me down. I'll be there and back in a blink." And off he went.

A quest. A wave. A mouse that's brave.

Lionel's little heart skipped with excitement. He pushed through brambles and thistles. He zigzagged through tall grass on his belly. Every now and then he poked his head up and glanced around. When dark clouds rolled above him, his ears twitched and his whiskers quivered. He heard a low rumbling in the distance.

A drip. A drop. An echoing plop!

Lionel tried to dart between raindrops. Soon he was drenched. And quite lost. Then the sound of ducks quacking drew him to the edge of a pond. And just beyond the pond was the dairy barn!

A soaker. A slosher. A fine-feather washer.

Lionel leapt onto a floating leaf. But a school of fish made the leaf boat swirl dizzily, knocking Lionel flat.

Clinging to the leaf, he kicked wildly with his rear paws. Finally he made it to the shore. Rain pelted Lionel from all sides.

He slogged up the bank and through the muddy pasture. Panting, he squeezed under the barn door.

"At last!" he cried. "The land of the brie! The home of the whey!"

"No cheese here," purred a voice. "But, I'd love a little mouse with my cream."

A spit. A spat. A sharp-clawed cat!

Lionel's heart froze. Then he sprang straight up to the tip of a cow's tail and held on for dear life. Lionel swung from one tail to the next until he landed high on a window ledge. Down below the cat paced back and forth.

Lionel's little heart thumped with fear.

A set of round yellowish eyes peered down from a rafter. "Hoot! Hoot!" said a barn owl. "I won't let that cat have you, you sweet little mouse."

"Oh, dear," said Lionel. "You'll have me for yourself!"

Lionel searched for an escape, but saw none. Above him the owl sharpened its beak on the rafter.

Owl above. Cat below. No place to go!

Lionel peered out the window as the thunder rumbled. *FLASH!* He jumped as lightning filled the sky. He lost his footing and clung to the windowsill by a single toenail.

A boom! A jolt! A lightning bolt!

CRASH! The wind blew the barn door open sending the startled owl out. Lionel couldn't hold on any longer! He tumbled to the barn floor and rolled right toward the waiting cat.

But a shadowy figure stood in the doorway.

En garde! Scat! Hit the road, cat!

With a yowl, the cat dashed away.

Lionel trembled as he peeked through his paws. His whiskers quivered. His black eyes blinked. At last he smiled whisker to whisker. "Pip?!?"

"Of course it's me," said Pip. "On a day like this, everyone needs an umbrella."

"Yes," said Lionel. "On a day like this everyone *does* need an umbrella. And a friend like you."

"Let's scurry home," said Pip.

"Yes, let's," said Lionel.

One tinkers. One studies. Best ever buddies. ∎

A Bucket Full of Dreams

by **Valarie Pearce** | illustrated by **Brian Parker**

Last night I had a dream.

I met a mysterious man with kind eyes and a gentle smile. In his hand he had a purple bucket.

The bucket was filled to the brim with bright and colorful stars that glittered and glowed: red, orange, yellow, green, blue, violet, silver, and gold!

I asked him, Sir, what is your name?

I am many things to many people, he answered, but most know me as The Dreamer.

Why? I asked.

He laughed. When I was young like you I dreamed of the world being many things.

As he spoke, the stars in his purple bucket began to shimmer and sparkle as if they were alive.

These stars, he said, represent each of my dreams.

I watched as The Dreamer delicately plucked out each star. He blew on each one as he placed them in the sky.

Then he called them by name: *Compassion* so hearts can agree. *Courage* to keep trying and never give up. *Friendship* so no one walks alone. *Generosity* so each of us lends the other a helping hand. And finally, *Brotherhood* so we remember we are all a part of a big family.

Suddenly, The Dreamer stopped speaking. I looked in his purple bucket.

You have no more stars! I cried.

The Dreamer smiled wide and brilliant. He took a deep breath and blew all the stars out into the cosmos. They leaped and danced and collided together, zipping and zinging and shaping into . . .

One BIG bright star.

What is it? I whispered.

But when I looked, The Dreamer was gone! All that was left was his purple bucket.

Carefully, I picked up the bucket and looked inside.

To my surprise it began to fill with stars! Lots and lots of stars: big stars, little stars, bright and bold stars. This time I did not have to ask. I knew what they were.

They were MY dreams.

Dreams to call my own. Dreams that snapped and shook and clapped! Dreams to fill up the world with, just as The Dreamer had.

I awoke from my sleep as happy and peaceful as could be.

I am the dreamer now and The Dreamer's dream . . . is me! ■

Diary of a Volcano

by **Elizabeth Rusch** | illustrated by **Mark Fearing**

1720 I can see why they call me Squirt. Sheesh! It's tough being the youngest AND the smallest in the family.

1750 Woke up this morning feeling *REALLY shaky.*

1751 Mmmm, melted rock for breakfast, my favorite! Melted rock for lunch . . . and dinner . . . and dessert . . . All right, all right, enough magma already! I'm *STUFFED!*

1751 Don't feel so good today. All that magma made me gassy. BURP! *Smells like rotten eggs. Pee-yew!*

1751 Think I'm getting a fever, now. Look at that: 1,000 degrees! Something weird is going on . . .

1751 Guess what? Lava tickles! Maybe *THAT'S* why they call me Squirt . . .

1753 That's what I call a growth spurt. Check out the dome I built. Ta-Da! I can skywrite, too! *WHEEEE!*

1760 Good news: I'm as big as the other volcanoes! Bad news: My magma is getting thicker and heavier. Got to . . . get this . . . big chunk . . . out. *ARRGH*, I can't do it. All this work is making me sleepy. *ZZzzz.*

2020 *YAWN.* That was a nice nap. ***WHOA!*** There are roads and farms and houses all over me! I must have slept a long time . . .

2031 Got that shaky feeling again. And I'm really full. Too full. Tried to burp, but nothing came out. I think I'm clogged up.

2031 Where's everyone going?

Shake, shake, shake!!!!!
Crack crash slide.

My Scrapbook

My first eruption

Some of my big brothers and sisters

Celebrating my first century

Cough! *COUGH! KA-POW!*

Wow! Guess I really blew my top this time . . .

2031 Took another peek in the lake today. I am *FILTHY!* Sheesh! And after all that work, I'm no taller than when I started! Pretty sleepy again, too. ZZzzz . . .

2580 Hello, world! Squirt here again. You didn't think I'd sleep forever, did you? No way. I've got more growing to do!

Author's Note

Volcanoes don't *really* keep diaries, but scientists do. By taking notes on lots of volcanoes over long periods of time, *volcanologists* have figured out that most active volcanoes go through cycles of sleeping, growing, and erupting. In fact, active volcanoes spend most of their time either asleep (dormant) or growing. Just like you! ■

Something Fishy

by **Trudy Ludwig** | illustrated by **Cathy Stever**

There's something fishy with those fish.
LOOK! See the way their tails go **SWISH?**

Those fish swim fast when we swim slow.
They even swim against the flow.

Their silver scales will turn to red.
Ours stay the same from tail to head.

Those fish grow big while we stay small.
They're simply not our kind at all!

Let's stay away from those strange fish.
They're not like us. Let's leave them — **SWISH!**

WAIT! What's that shadow over there?
It's coming closer . . . fish, **BEWARE!**

It's very big, with pointy teeth!
Where can we hide when there's no reef?

Those fish that aren't our kind swim near.
They swim toward us. They sense our fear.

For us those fish have formed a wall!
A wall that's wide, a wall that's tall!

We'll hide behind their wall and stay.
Let's hope that big seal goes away!

That hungry seal has now swum past.
It's safe to leave this wall at last.

Those fish are different, but they're kind.
Kind, helpful fish are hard to find.

There's nothing fishy with those fish.
Let's be their friends.

Let's join them — SWISH!

Fun Facts About "Those Fish"

✔ We are Chinook, or king salmon.
   We're the state fish of Oregon.

✔ We swim in freshwater streams and
   the saltwater ocean.

✔ When we feel threatened, we swim close together
   in one large group or "school," making it harder
   for predators to identify a single fish to go after.

✔ We're strong swimmers. As adult fish, we swim
   hundreds of miles to return to the streams and
   rivers where we were born to lay our eggs.

✔ We're big jumpers — jumping as high as
   7 to 10 feet up waterfalls and rivers to get
   back to our home streams.

✔ Our strong sense of smell and direction help
   us find our way.

✔ Our silver fish scales turn red when we're
   ready to lay eggs.

✔ We can grow up to 5 feet long and weigh
   as much as 110 pounds! ■

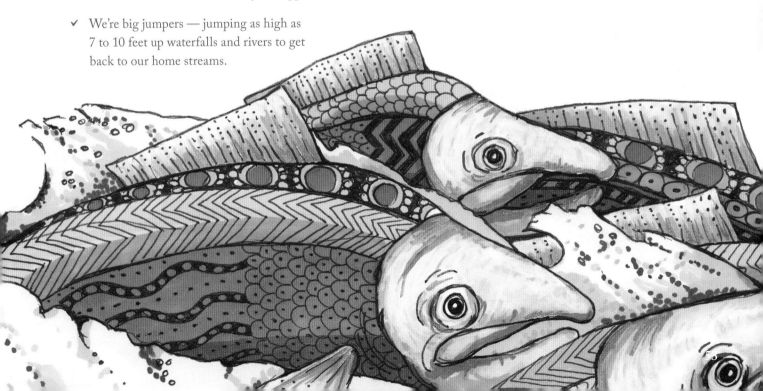

George Fletcher: The People's Champion

by **Amber J. Keyser** | illustrated by **Wendy Myers**

Pendleton Round-Up, Oregon, 1911

Horses stamp the dusty ground and snort. Muscles swirl under sleek coats. *They are ready to run.*

Cowboys polish bridles and buckle on chaps. Spurs jingle. Saddles shine. *They are ready to ride.*

The wooden stands are packed. White and Chinese. Nez Perce and Umatilla. Children clutch fry bread and rock candy. *They are ready to cheer.*

In a thunder of horse and rider, the competitors gallop into the arena and charge the stands. The crowd roars. *Let the Round-Up begin!*

The desert sun beats down on stagecoach races and steer roping, wild horse sprints and trick-riding. Finally, it's time for the big event — the Saddle Bronc Championship.

The rules are simple — grip the halter rope in one hand, keep the other in the air, and  stay in the saddle. The three cowboys in the final round are some of the best Pendleton has ever seen.

Nez Perce rider Jackson Sundown ties his long braids under his chin and secures his hat. He's tall and lean, a warrior who rode with Chief Joseph. His angora chaps ripple as the horse rears and swerves, ducks and dives. At first, it seems like a winning ride, but Sundown is thrown and disqualified.

Next up is John Spain, a white man who rides in Wild West shows. His silk scarf dances as the horse leaps and bucks. Boards splinter and crack when horse and rider crash into the wooden railing. The big cowboy keeps his seat, but his free hand dips toward the saddle. The crowd yells, "He pulled the leather!" But the judges declare the ride a clean one.

Last to ride is George Fletcher, a black cowboy who grew up near the Umatilla Reservation, catching wild mustangs and netting salmon at Celilo Falls. He's a natural rider with a big laugh and a big heart. The crowd loves him. "Let 'er buck!" they cheer, when he lets loose on a bronc named Sweeney.

The horse plunges and twists. Its hooves churn the dirt. On Sweeney's back, George Fletcher is loose and easy. His body flows with the herky-jerky movements of the horse. His right hand holds the rope. His left circles high overhead. He belongs on a horse like other folks belong on the ground.

When George Fletcher's ride is done, the crowd explodes. People cheer themselves hoarse. Children whistle and throw their hats in the air. The judges deliberate. Two men completed the ride. Their scores will depend on style and skill. When the judges send a slip of paper to the announcer, the crowd squirms in anticipation.

The announcer leans into the megaphone and booms over the stands, "The winner is . . . John Spain!" The crowd groans. Children boo. Murmurs swell like a river in flood. "George Fletcher rode the best," they say. "The judges don't want a black man to win."

They clap when John Spain receives the championship saddle worth $350, but 10,000 voices roar in unison when George Fletcher gallops into the arena on his little Cayuse pony. Every throat cheers. Every hand pounds. They want their hero rewarded for his skill.

A man in the stands takes charge. He asks George Fletcher for his black felt hat. With a sharp pocketknife, the man cuts the hat into pieces. "Five dollars! Five dollars for a piece of history!"

Men and women press forward. Each wants to touch the felt. They want to remember how George Fletcher flew over the earth. When every piece is claimed, the cowboy gets his winnings — $700!

Men hoist George Fletcher onto their shoulders for a victory lap. He waves and smiles. From high in the stands, a voice calls, "The People's Champion!" Other voices take up the thunderous chant.

People's Champion!
People's Champion!
George Fletcher is the People's Champion!

Historical Note

By 1910, the year of the first Pendleton Round-Up, the open ranges of the West had been mostly converted to farms and cities. The rodeo was to be a Wild West show that would celebrate the "old days" and showcase the skills of cowgirls, cowboys, and Native American riders. George Fletcher was one of the few free African Americans in the entire state because of Oregon's exclusion laws (1857–1926). He worked the rodeo circuit until World War I. Upon returning from Europe, he rode and ranched until his death in 1973. He is a member of the Pendleton Round-Up Hall of Fame, the National Cowboy Hall of Fame, and the National Cowboys of Color Hall of Fame. ■

Main source material and photo from: *Red White Black: A True Story of Race and Rodeo* by Rick Steber (2013)

Mount Tabor:
Home of Ardi the Squirrel

by **Estela Bernal** | illustrated by **Deborah Hocking**

Ardi the Squirrel loves to pop up everywhere in Mount Tabor Park. She especially loves to pester Luna, who visits the park every day.

If Luna plays tennis, Ardi scampers across the net.

"Scoot!" says Luna. ***Don't be a pest.***

If Luna is hiking and stops to check out Mount Hood, Ardi rifles through her binocular case looking for nuts.

"Shoo!" says Luna. ***Don't be a pest.***

If Luna walks her dogs, Ardi tries to lure them up a tree.

"Scram!" says Luna. ***Don't be a pest.***

If Luna climbs the summit to take pictures of the statue of Harvey Scott, Ardi dashes up to pose on his outstretched arm.

"Go away!" says Luna. ***Don't be a pest.***

Mt. St. Helens, an active volcano!

Restroom that looks like a fairytale cottage

HARVEY W. SCOTT

Reservoir

Tennis courts

Wild blackberries

Old growth Douglas Fir trees

Amphitheater

If Luna rides the merry-go-round at the playground, Ardi stands in the middle and spins.

"Get lost!" says Luna. ***Don't be a pest.***

If Luna goes to a concert in the park, Ardi scurries back and forth across the stage.

"¡Basta!" says Luna. ***Don't be a pest.***

One day, Ardi's not waiting by the gate. She's not chasing Luna at the dog park. She's not pestering her on the trail.

Where could Ardi be?

Luna hikes to the summit of Mount Tabor. She climbs up and down the stairs. She peeks under bushes and behind trees. But she can't find Ardi anywhere.

Tired and lonely, Luna leans against a tree. Then an acorn drops on her head.

Ardi!

But . . . Ardi's not alone. Behind her, inside a cozy knothole, are some baby Ardis. Luna counts them — one, two, three.

Now, when Luna goes to Mount Tabor, there are four Ardis waiting to welcome her, to pester her, to follow her everywhere.

And Luna's always happy to see them. ■

Glossary

Ardilla	*Ahr DEE yah*	Squirrel *(Ardi is short for Ardilla)*
¡Basta!	*BAHS tah*	Enough already!
Luna	*LOO nah*	Moon

Mt. Tabor summit: 636' It's an extinct volcano!

Mt. Hood   elevation: 11,249'

Great view of downtown Portland

Big Pink

Stairs that go all the way to the top!

Ardi!

Cliff here you see volcanic rock!

magnificent hiking trails

The Day the Puddles Stomped Back

by **Heidi Schulz** | illustrated by **Gesine Krätzner**

Last Saturday was the 54th rainy day in a row. I stared out the window and sighed.

"Oh for goodness' sake," my mom said, "go outside and play! Explore. Stomp in puddles. ***You live in Oregon! You won't melt if you get wet.***"

She handed me a jacket and pointed at the door. Mom was wearing her I-Mean-Business look, so I didn't even try to argue. I pulled on my rubber boots, then stood shivering in the shelter of our front porch.

I wasn't the only one out on Filbert Lane that morning. Across the street, Mrs. McElroy headed down her front walk to get her newspaper from where it lay soaking in a puddle. But this puddle wasn't acting normal.

Mrs. McElroy's puddle twitched. It trembled.

And just as Mrs. McElroy went to step around it, the puddle raised itself right up off the ground and . . .

SPLASH!

A column of water stomped Mrs. McElroy, knocking her into her prize-winning azaleas!

Down the street, Mr. Reyes was walking his twin teacup poodles, Curly Sue and Even Curlier Sue. The dogs stopped to sniff at a puddle on the sidewalk.

The puddle twitched, and trembled, and raised itself up . . . ***SPLASH!***

All the curl was stomped right out of those puddle-drenched poodles.

Jenny, our mail carrier, got out of her jeep to bring a few packages to the Rosen family's door, when an under-the-porch puddle twitched, and trembled, and raised itself up . . .

SPLASH!!!

It stomped Jenny right off her feet, scattering boxes everywhere.

In the street, right in front of my house, leaves had clogged the gutter, making a puddle the size of a tiny lake. If that one decided to attack, it could cause a small tsunami!

Under my gaze, the puddle twitched.

The entire neighborhood would be flooded!

It trembled.

Someone had to do something!

It started to raise itself up, but before it could get far, I ran down the porch steps, took a flying leap, and gave that puddle the biggest double-footed stomp Filbert Lane had ever seen!

Water splashed up, drenching me to the skin, but I didn't care. *I just kept stomping*.

The twitching and trembling stopped. It was working! "Everyone, stomp!" I yelled.

And thus began ***The Great Filbert Lane Puddle Battle***.

Mrs. McElroy pulled herself out of her azalea bushes and gave her puddle a mighty clomp.

Mr. Reyes, Curly Sue, and Even Curlier Sue romped through their puddle while laughing and barking wildly.

Jenny, the mail carrier, stood up, climbed onto her biggest package, let out a karate yell, and crashed down on her puddle.

I kept stomping my lake. "Take that!" I said. "And that!"

We made such a commotion that up and down the street, doors began to open. When they saw us stomping, the neighbors couldn't resist. Everyone pulled on rubber boots and joined the battle.

All seven Bowen sisters came out, carrying their baby brother. The baby toddled through a teeny-tiny puddle while the girls marched in a circle around him.

Old Mr. LeGrand threw down his cane, took Mrs. LeGrand by the hand, and performed a splashy tango on a puddle.

Jacob Johnson came outside still in his pajamas. Who knew teenagers wore *Star Wars* flannels? He flashed me a thumbs-up, yelled, "Cannonball!" and gave his driveway puddle a ***KER-SPLASH***.

My mom stood shivering on our porch. "C'mon, Mom!" I called. "We need your help. You live in Oregon! You won't melt if you get wet!"

I must have had on my I-Mean-Business face, because she sprinted off the porch and leapt into my lake, her laughing face turned up to the rain.

Once all the puddles stopped twitching and trembling, and we were sure we had shown them who was boss, Mom invited the whole street over to our house. I passed out towels, the oldest Bowen sister built a fire in the fireplace, and Mom gave everyone a steaming mug of hot cocoa, with extra marshmallows.

Ever since that day — the day of ***The Great Filbert Lane Puddle Battle*** — I keep a close eye on the puddles. So far there's been no more twitching, no more trembling.

But I'm through with taking chances.

On rainy days, I rush right outside and stomp every puddle in sight — before they have a chance to stomp me. ■

Old as Clouds, Wise as Wind

by **Gina Ochsner** | illustrated by **Mike Lawrence**

Once there was a man as old as clouds and wise as wind. If he had a name, no one knew it. He lived alone in his small workshop up on the hill. Inside, he made birds out of pieces of aluminum, bits of tin, the teeth of broken zippers. Coils from the backsides of refrigerators became rib cages. Wire coat hangers became wings. Silver gum wrappers and strips of colored fabric became feathers.

Each bird was built from whatever was on hand. No two birds looked alike.

The old man worked all day and sometimes well into the night. When he had made a bird to his satisfaction, he'd lift it gently to his face and whisper. As he whispered, the metal chests of his birds swelled. Their wings rustled. Then with one, two, three flaps of their wings, they lifted off his hand, soared out the open door, and curled into the sky like colored scarves.

The people in town brought the old man their metal scraps. Sometimes they brought questions, too. *"What makes your birds fly?"* they wondered. If a grown-up asked, the old man would smile an apology. But if a child asked, he would patiently explain:

> *"I tell the birds the words they need to hear, the right words to help them fly."*

Did he sell his amazing birds? No. He gave them away to anyone who asked.

"Love this bird. It is utterly unique. Help it to fly," he'd explain. People always promised to do just that. But sometimes promises wear thin. Occasionally, the old man would find one of his birds dumped in a trash can or lost in the forest. This made him sad.

One boy became a regular visitor. Day after day, week after week, he swept the metal shavings from the workshop floor. The old man complimented the boy on his hard work and reminded him:

"You are much loved, boy. You are utterly unique. Fly as only you can."

One day a stranger climbed the hill and knocked on the workshop door. Being old as clouds, wise as wind the old man could guess what this man wanted.

"I own a factory," the visitor said. "Together we could build many birds, hundreds of them." The man's eyes were like charcoal and his voice was like soot.

"Some things are not meant to be bought or sold," the old man answered.

"But I could make you rich!" the factory owner said.

But the old man did not want money. He just wanted to make his birds. And so, the old man smiled and ushered the visitor out the door.

For many weeks and months the old man and his apprentice bent wire and twisted metal. Together they fastened wings to rib cages, feathers to wings. They built and released brightly colored birds that filled the air with their beautiful music.

The apprentice loved the old man very much. He saw how poorly the old man lived: he had almost no food and he wore the same ragged clothes day after day. The apprentice couldn't help thinking that the factory owner's ideas weren't such bad ones.

One day the apprentice approached the old man. "I would like to go away and see the world." The old man nodded sadly and watched his apprentice go.

Months passed. The old man began to worry. He gathered up his burlap sack and went to the woods. There he discovered something strange: metal birds broken and scattered across the forest floor. They all looked precisely the same and not a single one had a bit of color.

Because he was old as clouds, wise as wind, the old man kept walking. He knew when something needed to be found and fixed. Sure enough he came across his apprentice, slumped against a tree.

"Why haven't you come back?" the old man asked.

"I am too ashamed," the apprentice said. His voice was hollow like the chests of the broken metal birds.

The old man pulled the boy to his feet. *"Come back anyway."*

When they reached the workshop, the apprentice stopped at the door. "I sold your design. But the birds we made couldn't fly well and crashed."

The old man placed a wire coil in the apprentice's left hand. "Why did they fall?"

"Because I didn't know the right words to make them fly."

The old man placed a pair of pliers in the apprentice's right hand. "They are words you've heard many times."

The old man led the boy back into his workshop, then whispered in his ear:

"You are much loved, boy. You are utterly unique. Fly as only you can." ∎

Moon Song

by **Barbara Herkert** | illustrated by **Johanna Wright**

One blue-black night
in the Northwest sky,
silver Moon rose
round and bright.

A pale outsider stood
alone among the pines,
the midnight renegade,
Coyote.

Darkness disappeared
as he stepped
into Moon's glow.
"Enchanting," said Coyote.

Moon beamed at the night rover
and sang a silver note.
***Coyote raised his snout
to sing along.***

The silent forest stirred.
Hare loped after Squirrel
who bounded after Doe,
lured by the dazzling duet.

Quail bobbed to the clearing,
Raccoon waddled into sight,
Mouse pitter-pattered
to the lunar melody.

Coyote's call soared
into the indigo night.
*"Oooh, ooh-ooh-oooh,
Moooon Song."*

Coyote yip-yip-yipped.
He yow-yow-yowled.
Porcupine sputtered,
"It's spellbinding."

"Foo-hoo-hoo-lish," Owl hooted.
"He's a lunatic!" Bat squeaked.
"Moonstruck!"
the other animals agreed.

The weary woodland creatures
slipped beneath the canopy
while Coyote and Moon
crooned 'til dawn.

Each evening Coyote
padded to the forest edge.
**But Moon turned her face
a little more each night.**

"Come back," Coyote pleaded.
"I will return," Moon said.
She winked at him with
one last silver sliver.

Now old Coyote waits
amid the feathery pines
for his companion to arise,
round and bright.

Then the outlaw lifts his snout
and sings a moonlit strain.
*"Oooh, ooh-ooh-oooh,
Moooon Song."*

Next time you hear Coyote,
look closely at full Moon.
She is singing an
alluring harmony.

If you're moon-hearted,
you might like to sing along.
*"Oooh, ooh-ooh-oooh,
Moooon Song."*

Author's Note

Moon and Coyote have inspired myths, folklore, and
superstition. Moon has been worshiped as well as held
responsible for "lunatic" behavior. Coyote's curiosity
and mischief often lead to trouble; he is mistrusted and
misunderstood. In many stories, Moon feels alone in
the heavens. I like to think of Coyote's night song as a
kinship with Moon, two outsiders who find comfort in
each other. ∎

Paw-sitively Yummy

by **Bart King** | illustrated by **Carolyn Conahan**

It was a hot summer day as Beatrice and Raj pedaled down the street.

"There sure are lots of bikes out today!" said Bea.

"Hey, look at that one!" said Raj. A man rode by on a bike that was really tall. *It stretched up and up and UP.*

"Howdy, down there," he called.

Bea wondered if he had to climb a ladder to get on his seat.

Another bike went by. This one looked like a wheelbarrow with pedals! A woman pedaled it, and a little girl with flowers on her bike helmet sat in front. The girl waved to Bea and Raj as she passed by.

Then Bea's parents pedaled up. There were on a bike with two seats and pedals for both of them, one behind the other.

"Anyone else hear music?" asked Bea's mom.

It was true. Music floated on the summer breeze. "The ice cream bike!" they yelled.

"We'll race you there!" said Bea's parents. ***And off they pedaled!***

As Bea licked her cool ice cream, she noticed something. The ice cream bike's music was like magic. As soon as people heard it, they came walking or running or rolling! Bea also noticed a man with his dog. The dog looked hopefully at the ice cream, but nobody gave him any.

"Poor doggy," said Bea. "Yeah, too bad he doesn't get anything," said Raj, gulping down the last of his ice cream sandwich.

Suddenly, Bea had an idea!

She raced home, said hello to her dog, Winston, then grabbed Winston's dog whistle. "What are you doing?" asked Raj.

"You'll see," said Bea. First she tied the whistle to her handlebars. Then she attached panniers to her bike. She used these to carry her books to school.

Raj frowned. "What are those for? School doesn't start for a month."

"I know," said Bea, pouring something into the panniers. She was ready to go!

"Listen for the music," said Bea as they headed back out to the street. At that moment, a song came piping through the air. The two friends looked at each other. "Ice cream!" they yelled.

Bea grabbed the dog whistle. As she rode toward the music, she blew on it.

Can you guess what happened next? ■

Kip and the Great Food Cart Feud

by **Dale E. Basye** | illustrated by **Carolyn Garcia**

After school, Kip Zwicky helped run his family's Swiss food cart, Fondue 4 You, in downtown Portland.

Kip's favorite job was to stir the pots of bubbling cheese ***just right***. No matter what went into the pot, it always tasted good (except maybe that time he dropped an old Twinkie in).

Kip also loved the Vittle Village Food Court where their cart was parked. The exotic smells, the zesty flavors, and the fascinating chefs made every day deliciously different!

One day, however, ***everything turned sour.***

A new cart — Yum Kippur! — moved in next to Falafelly Good. Their hot matzo ball soup and steaming potato latkes caused a customer commotion on cold winter mornings.

Yum Kippur!'s sudden success also caused a commotion with the other carts. Falafelley Good's business slowed to a trickle. Until they started a two-for-one Tabouli special. Suddenly, Yum Kippur! wasn't doing so well, so they fought back with a Better Latke Than Never promotion and business boomed.

This was the beginning of the Great Food Cart Feud!

Wurst Case Scenario plotted to take over Papa's Got a Brand New Baguette. Dressed to Kielbasa hid its garbage behind I Can't Believe It's Not Haggis. And Between a Wok and a Hot Plate joined forces with Vietnom-nom to spread nasty rumors about Curry-ocity Killed the Cat!

Soon, every cart was in the battle. The tension was so thick you could cut it with a plastic knife. Or chopsticks. Or with your hands, like at Finger Food Fandango.

This is terrible! thought Kip. *Everyone is acting crazy.*

Kip gathered together his best friends — Yael, whose family owned Yum Kippur!, and Sabri, whose family ran Falafelly Good.

"We've got to do something about this feuding . . . it's really heating up!" Kip said.

"Totally. It stinks more than In Cod We Trust in the summer!" agreed Yael.

"We could be, like . . . the United Nations!" said Sabri. "You know, bring peace to the carts!"

"Yes! We could be the United *Noshes*," Kip said. "And I think I have a peace plan. First we need to call an all-cart meeting at breakfast tomorrow."

"They won't come if it's just us kids asking," said Sabri.

"What if we said it was a mandatory meeting with the Department of Health?" suggested Yael. "Then they'd *have* to come."

"Great idea!" Kip said. "And once everyone is together, we'll make them work things out."

Though Sabri and Yael were doubtful Kip's plan would work, it was the only plan they had. So they raced off to make flyers, and posted them on each and every cart.

It was dark and stormy outside as the cart owners entered the big Special Events tent. But it was even stormier *inside!* Everyone sat fuming at one another, plotting and whispering in their native languages. They each had their own breakfasts, which they barely touched.

Kip swallowed nervously as he climbed onto a table. The lights flickered as the old generator sputtered.

"The Health Inspector couldn't be here today because he, uh . . . got sick," Kip said, the lights flickering again. "Instead, I thought we could spend the time talking about the trouble we've been having here at Vittle Village."

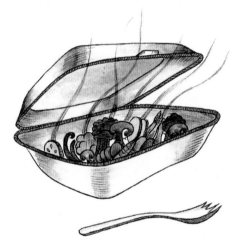

The crowd grumbled. Angry cart owners pushed back their chairs and started to leave. Sabri and Yael sighed. The plan wasn't working!

Suddenly, the lights went out, leaving everyone in darkness. It was impossible to see the doorway, so people sat back down to wait for the lights to come back on. Their empty bellies began growling. This gave Kip an idea. He whispered to Sabri and Yael, *"Switch everyone's food."*

"Why?" they whispered back.

"Trust me. Switch the food."

The United Noshes jumped into action: in the dark they crept from table to table and switched breakfasts. The sleepy cart owners began to eat.

The owners of Falafelly Good ate bagels, cream cheese, and lox. The Yum Kippur! folks ate freshly baked flatbread with salty goat cheese and olives. The Vietnom-nom chef ate sausages and hot rolls with marmalade while the owner of Wurst Case Scenario ate sticky rice with egg.

The lights came back on.

As the cart chefs realized they were eating the wrong food, they scowled. But slowly they began to smile as they savored the exotic yet mouth-watering foods. Soon, everyone relaxed and began chatting with one another like old friends. They asked their neighbors how their breakfasts were made, where the recipes came from, and what were the secret ingredients. The cart owners were clearing the air while they were clearing their plates!

"I guess it's true: variety really is the spice of life," said Sabri.

"*And the way to a person's heart is through their stomach,*" added Yael.

"I guess we served them just what they needed," said Kip. "Food for thought!" ∎

A Really Good Present for Dad

by **Barbara Kerley** | illustrated by **Carolyn Conahan**

The day before Father's Day, I tell my big brother JJ, "We need to get Dad a really good present."

JJ flips a page in his comic book. "I already have one: a buy-one-get-one-free coupon for milkshakes."

"Where'd you get money for that?" I ask, because he's as broke as I am.

"Don't need money when you have a coupon, Toby." He shakes his head. "Dad only has to buy mine. His will be free."

That doesn't seem like a very good present to me.

I talk it over with Bowser. "Dad likes hiking, and he likes relaxing in his easy chair. But no way can I buy him new hiking boots or a new chair. What should I get him?"

Bowser just drools and scratches his ear. "A lotta help you are," I say.

I think about it all day, and by bedtime, I've figured it out. "We have to go out tomorrow to get your present," I tell Dad when he comes into our room to say goodnight. "And we have to go out early."

"How early?" JJ asks.

"Early. Before breakfast." JJ pulls his pillow over his face. I set my alarm.

When the alarm goes off the next morning, it's barely light out. "Ugh," JJ groans, but he gets up because it's Father's Day.

Downstairs, Dad is drinking coffee. "Time to go? Do I need my car keys?"

"We're walking," I say. "But bring your phone."

"Who would we call?" JJ grumbles "No one's up this early."

Bowser is excited. I hang on to his leash as he pulls me across the park to the trail that runs through the Oaks Bottom Wildlife Refuge.

"Hiking! My favorite!" Dad says. "Thanks, Toby!"

"That's not your present."

Birds are chirping. Squirrels are racing. Bowser barks at them all. Along the trail is marsh filled with long reeds. There are paths through the reeds like little roads in the still water. Every time we see one, I stop to look.

"Why do we keep stopping?" JJ complains.

"Shhh . . ." I whisper.

Around a bend, the reeds open up into a quiet stretch of water. And there, finally, I find what I'm looking for: a family of ducks with four fuzzy ducklings!

"Hand me your phone," I whisper to Dad.

"You're calling the ducks?" JJ mutters.

"I'm taking their picture to put on the wall by Dad's chair." I turn to Dad. "Then you can think about hiking while you're relaxing. That's the present."

"Great idea!" Dad whispers. I hand him the leash as he hands me the phone.

But just as I crouch down to get a good shot, Bowser lunges at the ducks. He knocks me over as I'm pushing the button.

CRASH! SPLASH! QUACK!

The ducks splash into the reeds to hide, and Bowser splashes in after them. Before I can take another picture, the ducks are gone.

When we check the phone, all the picture shows is brown smudges, a big splash, and the muddy tip of Bowser's tail.

"I got up early for that?" JJ says. My shoulders slump.

"I liked the hiking part," Dad says as we head back up the trail.

JJ is walking fast. He is probably thinking how happy Dad will be when he gives him the milkshake coupon. Dad and Bowser are next, then me, my feet dragging.

When we reach the park, Dad puts his arm across my shoulders. Our hike is almost over. Next year, I will think of a really good present.

"You can delete that stupid picture," I tell him. He gives my shoulder a squeeze.

But then, I see a guy walking his dog, and suddenly I know just what to do. I grab Dad's hand and start to run. "Come on, JJ!"

I race up to the guy and say, "Can you take our picture?"

When we get home, JJ runs upstairs to get the coupon, a big smile on his face. But I'm happy, too. Because after breakfast, I print out the picture and pin it up right above Dad's easy chair. "Now that," says Dad, "is a really good present." ∎

Serafina's Tree

by **Judy Cox** | illustrated by **Zoey Abbott Wagner**

Serafina and Mrs. Juarez shared a tree. It grew between their houses in Portland — a big plum tree so old even Mrs. Juarez didn't remember when it was planted. "It's been here since I was a girl," she told Serafina.

In spring, the tree was lacy with blossoms. "Like my wedding dress!" said Mrs. Juarez.

By summer, the plums were red and ripe. Mrs. Juarez held the ladder steady. Serafina reached way up to pick the plums. They filled a whole basket.

"We'll make plum preserves," said Mrs. Juarez.

Mrs. Juarez showed Serafina how to mash the plums. Her fingernails were painted as red as the juicy plums. The veins on her hands were blue, like roads on a map.

When the jars were full, Serafina set them on the windowsill. The yellow preserves sparkled in the sunlight. "Liquid gold. That's what my husband used to say." Mrs. Juarez smacked her lips.

One hot afternoon, Serafina and Mrs. Juarez set a table in the shade under the plum tree. They spooned preserves on triangles of toast.

"Mmmm," said Serafina. ***"Tastes like summer."***

In autumn, the wind whisked plum leaves into whirlwinds. Serafina twirled in her new plaid school dress. Mrs. Juarez twirled too, but slowly. "It's my arthritis," she explained. "I can't twirl like I used to."

In winter, the tree's bare branches sparkled with frost. "Like the Snow Queen's crown," Mrs. Juarez said. "Soon we'll see the buds again. She raked dead leaves from the frozen ground. Serafina held the compost bin.

One day, Mrs. Juarez didn't come outside. Serafina peered out of her kitchen window, watching.

"She has a bad cold," said Mom, putting down the phone. "Let's take her some chicken soup."

The soup didn't help. A week later, an ambulance came. Serafina watched the paramedics wheel Mrs. Juarez out. She looked tiny in her white nightdress.

Overhead, the winter sky was blue. "Look, Mrs. Juarez," said Serafina. *"Our tree is budding."*

Mrs. Juarez patted Serafina's hand. "Take good care of our tree until I come home," she said. The ambulance drove away. The yard looked bare. Serafina slowly walked inside.

Soon the plum tree was white with blossoms again. Serafina took a branch when she visited Mrs. Juarez in the hospital.

"They're sending me to a care center," said Mrs. Juarez. Tears dribbled down her cheeks. "How can I leave my house?" She wiped her eyes. Serafina had a lump in her throat.

"Why can't Mrs. Juarez come home?" she asked Mom as they drove away.

"She's too frail to care for herself," said Mom. "In the care center, they have a wheelchair."

"She could have a wheelchair at home."

"They have doctors to treat her if she gets sick."

"We could call the doctor if she gets sick."

"Honey, I know it's sad, but Mrs. Juarez needs people to help her all day and all night. She'll get good care at the center."

"Can we visit?"

Mom squeezed Serafina's hand. "Of course."

Spring passed into summer. Serafina went to the plum tree every day. The tiny, green plums swelled. The hot sun turned them red and yellow.

She visited Mrs. Juarez at the care center. "It's a good place," said Mrs. Juarez. "There's a group of folks here who play a mean hand of bridge. But I miss our tree. Are the plums ripe yet?" She closed her eyes. *"Mmmm, I can taste them now."*

When Serafina got home, she picked a bushel basket of plums. Without Mrs. Juarez to hold the ladder, she could only reach the lowest branches. She took the basket into her kitchen.

"Let's make preserves," she told Mom.

Mom laughed. "Oh, honey! I don't know how!"

"But I do," said Serafina.

Mom looked at her. "Are you sure?"

Serafina closed her eyes and pictured Mrs. Juarez peeling the plums and pitting them, adding sugar, mashing them up. "Yes," she said. "I'm sure."

They cooked the preserves, ladled them into glass jars, and sealed them with paraffin. Serafina set them on the windowsill. Sunlight streamed through the jars. *"Like liquid gold,"* she said.

They took a jar of preserves to Mrs. Juarez the next day. Serafina wheeled her chair into the courtyard. Mom set out tea and toast.

Mrs. Juarez spread a spoonful of preserves on the toast. She took a bite, closed her eyes. When she opened them, her eyes were wet. "Thank you, Serafina," she said. "You've brought me summer!"

How to Make Mrs. Juarez' Plum Preserves

- ✓ Gather a basket of soft, ripe plums.
- ✓ Wash well, peel, pit, and chop into chunks.
- ✓ Mix with ½ cup of sugar for every 1 cup of chopped plums.
- ✓ Cook the sugar and plums on low heat until it comes to a boil. Stir so it doesn't stick to the bottom of the pan.
- ✓ When the mixture reaches a rolling boil, let it cook for five minutes, stirring constantly so the mixture doesn't scorch.
- ✓ Let it cool. Skim off any foam and discard. Stir in 1 tablespoon of lemon juice. Ladle the preserves into clean, dry jars and seal with paraffin.

Enjoy! ■

Waffles

by **Eric A. Kimmel** | illustrated by **Kate Berube**

Bart and Blake got up early one Saturday morning.

"I'm hungry!" said Blake. "I want breakfast."

"We have to wait till Mom and Dad wake up," said Bart.

"But I'm hungry NOW!!!" said Blake.

"Have some cereal," said Bart.

"I hate cereal," said Blake.

"Have some eggs," said Bart.

"I hate eggs," said Blake.

"What do you want?" said Bart.

"I want waffles!" said Blake.

"Okay," said Bart. "Let's make waffles."

"How do you make waffles?" asked Blake.

"I know how," said Bart. "First we need the waffle iron."

"It's way up there on the top shelf," said Blake.

"Let's get it," said Bart.

Bart climbed on top of the kitchen counter. Then he climbed up on the lowest shelf. He stretched way, way up. He couldn't quite reach the waffle iron, but he reached the waffle iron cord. Bart pulled the cord. The waffle iron slid off the shelf. *Thump! Crash! Bump!* So did some other things.

"Catch!" Bart yelled.

"Got it!" said Blake. "What's next?"

"First we heat up the waffle iron," said Bart. Blake plugged in the cord. "We'll mix the ingredients while it gets hot. We need a mixing bowl."

84

Thump! Crash! Bump!

Blake got a mixing bowl. "What's next?"

"We need flour," said Bart.

"How much?" said Blake.

"About so much," said Bart.

Blake poured "about so much" flour into the bowl. "Now we need eggs, butter, and milk," said Bart. Blake got eggs, butter, and milk from the refrigerator.

Plop! Splash! Splat!

"How many eggs do we need?" asked Blake.

"About six or seven," said Bart. Blake dropped a stick of butter into the bowl.

He broke "about six or seven" eggs in, too. At least, he thought it was six or seven. He lost count in the middle.

"Now the milk," said Bart.

"We need about so much." Blake poured "about so much" milk into the bowl. "That's a lot of milk," he said.

"You need a lot of milk to make waffles," Bart told him. "Now we need sugar and baking powder. That's what makes the waffles get big."

"How much do we need?" asked Blake.

"About so much," said Bart.

Blake poured in sugar and baking powder. "Is that enough?" he asked.

"Maybe a little more," said Bart.

"Hey! What about the huckleberries we picked with Mom up on Mount Hood? I love huckleberry pancakes," said Blake.

"Pour them all in," said Bart. "That looks about right."

Blake stirred the flour, the milk, the butter, the butter wrapper, the sugar, the baking powder, the eggs, and some of the egg shells all together. "I'm getting tired. This is hard work."

"Let me stir," said Bart.

Blake and Bart took turns stirring until everything in the bowl was all mixed up. "Now we pour the mix onto the waffle maker. We're almost done," said Bart.

"Huckleberry waffles, yum! I can't wait!" said Blake.

Bart and Blake poured the mix onto the waffle maker. *"This is going to be SOME waffle!"* said Bart.

"Won't Mom and Dad be surprised!" said Blake. They certainly were.

So were the neighbors. ■

KIDS SHARE

WHAT IS YOUR FAVORITE THING ABOUT LIVING IN OREGON?

Playing in the rain

By Liam Andrews, 8 years old

The beautiful coast

By Kylie Morrow-Gilmore, 9 years old

POP QUIZ
Answer these questions from the book.
THE LETTERS UNDERLINED IN GREEN REVEAL A SECRET WORD!

1. The birds that nest in the Chapman Elementary School chimney every September are called:

___ ___ ___ ___ ___ ___
   ★

2. The state fish of Oregon is the:

___ ___ ___ ___ ___ ___ ___ ___ ___ ___ ___ ___
                                    ★

3. On Father's Day, JJ and his brother go hiking at a wildlife refuge called:

___ ___ ___ ___ ___ ___ ___ ___
   ★

4. The 1911 Pendleton Round-Up's People's Champion was:

___ ___ ___ ___ ___
___ ___ ___ ___ ___ ___
                  ★

5. Ardi the Squirrel plays with Luna at:

___ ___ ___ ___ ___ ___ ___ ___
         ★

AND THE SECRET WORD IS:

_____

89

Our Contributors

All of the contributors to *Oregon Reads Aloud* reside in the Pacific Northwest! We asked them to tell us something interesting about themselves. Here are their answers.

Dale E. Basye
wherethebadkidsgo.com
Author *Kip and the Great Food Cart Feud*

I always found Roald Dahl books wickedly funny. Conversely, I was a big fan of the *Little House* books, which are neither wicked nor funny.

OTHER WORKS: *Heck: Where the Bad Kids Go; Rapacia: The Second Circle of Heck; Blimpo: The Third Circle of Heck*

Estela Bernal
estelabernal.com
Author *Mount Tabor: Home of Ardi the Squirrel*

If I had to be anything other than an author, I'd want to be a veterinarian or a pediatrician because I love animals and children. Or better yet, a writer/vet like one of my all-time favorites, James A. Wight (better known as James Herriot).

OTHER WORKS: *Can You See ME Now?*

Carmen T. Bernier-Grand
carmenberniergrand.com
Author *Where Is My Mami?*

I like that Oregon has the smallest river (D River), the smallest park (Mill Ends Park), the smallest city (Greenhorn), and the smallest author of children and young adult books who has a "T" for Tall as part of her name.

OTHER WORKS: *César: Sí, se puede! / Yes, We Can; Shake It, Morena!; Diego: Bigger Than Life*

Kate Berube
kateberube.com
Illustrator *Waffles*

I've always loved to make things. So, all my favorite toys were things I made. I took shoe boxes and turned them into doll houses — and made furniture out of bits of cardboard. And for the tiny dolls that lived in the houses, I made clothes out of fabric scraps.

OTHER WORKS: *Hannah and Sugar; The Summer Nick Taught His Cats to Read; My Little Half Moon*

Susan Blackaby
susanblackaby.com
Author *The Camp Cook*

My dad's family is from Jordan Valley and he grew up in Ontario where I spent lots of summer vacations. So it is no surprise that my favorite places in Oregon are the gulches, craters, and creeks of the Owyhee country, easily accessed only by bighorn sheep, golden eagles, and sagebrush buttercups.

OTHER WORKS: *Brownie Groundhog and the February Fox; Brownie Groundhog and the Wintry Surprise; The Twelve Days of Christmas in Oregon*

Susan Boase
susanboase.com
Illustrator *Lionel and Pip*

If I couldn't be an author/illustrator, I would be a surgeon, because I am fascinated by the human body and how it all works.

OTHER WORKS: *Lucky Boy; Three Little Robbers; Peter Peter Picks a Pumpkin House*

Addie Boswell
addieboswell.com
Author & Illustrator *Go, Bikes, Go!*

I did not learn how to ride a bike when I was a kid, since I lived on a farm and was surrounded by gravel roads. When I started biking as a grown-up, I wasn't very good at turning corners!

OTHER WORKS: *The Rain Stomper*

Cathy Camper
cathycamper.com
Author *Meshmesh on Wheels*

I would like to learn how to analyze handwriting. It would be fun to try to unravel what people are like by reading their grocery lists.

OTHER WORKS: *Bugs Before Time; Prehistoric Insects and Their Relatives; Lowriders in Space*

Curtis C. Chen
curtiscchen.com
Author *Have Spacesuit, Will Travel*

If I could have any superpower, it would be flying. Anyone who tells you they'd rather be invisible is not to be trusted.

OTHER WORKS: *Waypoint Kangaroo;* A story in *2016 Young Explorer's Adventure Guide;* A story in *Mission: Tomorrow*

Nancy Coffelt
nancycoffelt.com
Author & Illustrator
Raccoon's Tooth

I love silly jokes. I used to have a dachshund named Dutch. My favorite thing to say to him was, "Hey, Dutch. Why the long face?" Get it — long nose — long face?

OTHER WORKS: *Big, Bigger, Biggest!; Fred Stays with Me!; Aunt Ant Leaves through the Leaves*

Carolyn Conahan
carolyndigbyconahan.com
Illustrator *A Really Good Present for Dad* and *Paw-sitively Yummy*

One year at Christmas, I told my grandfather I wanted to be an artist when I grew up because I loved to draw. He said, "But what if you had an accident and lost your hands? What would you do?" You might think he was trying to make me consider more sensible occupations. But no. He told me I should learn to draw with my feet, just in case. So I spent Christmas break gripping pencils with my toes.

OTHER WORKS: Staff artist for *Cricket Magazine; This Old Van; The Big Wish*

Judy Cox
judycox.net
Author *Serafina's Tree*

I play the U-bass (bass ukulele) in a rock-and-roll band, and the ukulele in a vintage jazz duo.

OTHER WORKS: *Snow Day for Mouse; Happy Birthday, Mrs. Millie!; Carmen Learns English*

Melissa Delzio
meldel.com
Designer *Oregon Reads Aloud*

My favorite toy as a kid was a giant, semi-broken video camera that held an entire VHS tape (ask your parents what that was). My brother, friends, and I would write, direct, and star in our own movies, commercials, and "magic" shows!

OTHER WORKS: *Our Portland Story Volumes I and II; Brain Food Children's Activity Deck*

Mark Fearing
markfearing.com
Illustrator *Diary of a Volcano*

I was NOT a big reader as a young student. I know, I know. I'm not supposed to say that. But I grew up on a farm alongside a river with lots of stuff to do. I also liked drawing and making animated films and sculpture.

OTHER WORKS: *The Three Little Aliens and the Big Bad Robot; Dilly Dally Daisy; The Great Thanksgiving Escape*

Carolyn Garcia
Illustrator *Kip and the Great Food Cart Feud*

Drawing makes me feel like I am floating, and I often lose track of time when I'm working on a piece of art. Sometimes hours go by and I don't even realize it! I also love to sing, play the accordion, and bake empanadas.

OTHER WORKS: *Moonboy*

Elizabeth Goss
lizabethgoss.com
Illustrator *Kira's Imagineering*

I would really like to try keeping honeybees. I think bees are marvelous, and I would love to watch them up close.

OTHER WORKS: *Bulfinch; Otherworldies*

Kim Griswell
kimgriswell.com
Author *Will and the Piper*

When I was about four years old, I had a doll that was as big as me. The doll could stand by itself and had strawberry blonde hair like I did. I sometimes dressed the doll in my clothes. One day, as my mother was rushing out the door, she grabbed the doll by the hand and said, "Let's go, Kim. We're late!" I thought my mom mistaking a doll for me was hysterically funny.

OTHER WORKS: *Rufus Goes to School; Rufus Goes to Sea; Uncle John's The Enchanted Toilet*

Barbara Herkert
barbaraherkert.com
Author *Moon Song*

My favorite part of the state is Central Oregon. I love the night sky! My story in this collection was inspired by one night at our cabin.

OTHER WORKS: *Sewing Stories: Harriet Powers' Journey from Slave to Artist; Mary Cassatt: Extraordinary Impressionist Painter*

Robin Herrera
robinherrera.com
Author *Dear Bigfoot*

Things that make me laugh are the sounds that zebras make and Bigfoot jokes.

OTHER WORKS: *Hope Is a Ferris Wheel*

Deborah Hocking
deborahhockingillustration.com
Illustrator *Mount Tabor: Home of Ardi the Squirrel*

If I wasn't a writer/illustrator, I would love to be a nurse and work with Doctors Without Borders, because the work they do is so very important and inspiring.

OTHER WORKS: *Build, Beaver, Build!*

David Hohn

davidhohn.com
Illustrator *The Camp Cook*

I don't like the taste of zucchini.

OTHER WORKS: *Finding Fairies: Secrets for Attracting Little People from Around the World; The Blanket Show; Zachary Zormer: Shape Transformer*

Barbara Kerley

barbarakerley.com
Author *A Really Good Present for Dad*

One of my favorite things to do in Oregon is to bike down the Springwater Corridor just as it's getting dark. Across the river, you can see all the lights of the city, but on the trail itself, it's quiet and peaceful. Sometimes you can even hear frogs chirping in the marshy forest. At that time of day, riding a bike is magical.

OTHER WORKS: *A Home for Mr. Emerson; With a Friend by Your Side; The Dinosaurs of Waterhouse Hawkins*

Robin Kerr

illustriousplay.com
Illustrator *Where Is My Mami?*

I love to see little kids who have obviously dressed themselves because they mix up layers like frilly dresses with cowboy boots and stripy tights and swimming suits. These fashionistas are frequently featured in my drawings.

OTHER WORKS: *The Big Rig; Raspberry Fizz; I Love Colors*

Amber J. Keyser

amberjkeyser.com
Author *George Fletcher: The People's Champion*

As a kid, my constant companion was a teddy bear called Cucumber. By the time I was four, I had picked all the fur off of him and eaten it. Yup. That's right. I ate the fur, and now I have a bald teddy bear named after my favorite vegetable.

OTHER WORKS: *An Algonquin Heart Song: Paddle My Own Canoe; Sneaker Century: A History of Athletic Shoes; The Way Back from Broken*

Eric A. Kimmel

ericakimmel.com
Author *Waffles*

I have a pet corn snake named Pirate. He's about 4.5 feet long and still growing. I'm glad he's friendly.

OTHER WORKS: *Rattlestiltskin; The Runaway Tortilla; Little Red Hot*

Bart King

bartking.net

Author *Paw-sitively Yummy*

I wish I had the power to turn "creamy" peanut butter into "chunky." Creamy is lame!

OTHER WORKS: *The Drake Equation; The Big Book of Superheroes; The Pocket Guide to Mischief*

Jane Kirkpatrick

jkbooks.com

Author *Sara Gets SMART*

When I was a kid I had a series of health problems that resulted in surgeries and one left me without a belly button. Instead I have a long scar that looks like a railroad track running across my middle. I'm thinking of putting a tattoo of a train on it.

OTHER WORKS: *The Memory Weaver; A Light in the Wilderness*

Gesine Krätzner

gesinekratzner.com

Illustrator *The Day the Puddles Stomped Back*

I love being in the water. So, if I had a superpower, I wish I could breathe under water and be a really good swimmer, like an otter. I'd be Otter Woman.

Mike Lawrence

mlawrenceillustration.com

Illustrator *Old as Clouds, Wise as Wind*

I hate to admit it, but I'm a sucker for a good fart joke! Also, I was once almost hit by lightning.

OTHER WORKS: *Muddy Max: The Mystery of Marsh Creek; The Incredible Adventures of Cinnamon Girl; Star Scouts (forthcoming)*

Trudy Ludwig

trudyludwig.com

Author *Something Fishy*

I'd love to have the ability to converse in any language spoken throughout the world. How fun would it be to travel anywhere and make new friends with people so different from me and then find out what we have in common!

OTHER WORKS: *The Invisible Boy; My Secret Bully; Confessions of a Former Bully*

Damien Macalino

macalino.com

Co-author *The Legend of the Mountains' Quarrel*

I wrote my first book in second grade during class, then brought it home, and talked my dad into publishing it.

OTHER WORKS: *What If an Alligator Ate an Avalanche?; Super Moo*

Heléna Macalino

macalino.com

Co-author *The Legend of the Mountains' Quarrel*

If I weren't a writer, I would be a person who raises bunnies and makes lots of money off of it, because I love bunnies and I've always wanted one. And my evil parents won't let me have one.

OTHER WORKS: *The Reflection; The Wish Fish*

Abigail Marble

abigailmarble.com
Illustrator *First Day Jitters*

I can write accurately upside down and backwards!

OTHER WORKS: *Two for Joy; Love Your Heart; My Secret Bully*

Michelle McCann

Editor *Oregon Reads Aloud*

My favorite place in Oregon (and maybe the world) is Mount Hood. Mostly because I love to snowboard, which I've been doing for almost 30 years. If I wasn't a kids' book editor, I would want to be a professional snowboarder. A 30-years-younger professional snowboarder!

OTHER WORKS: *Finding Fairies; Luba: The Angel of Bergen-Belsen; Girls Who Rocked the World*

Natalie Metzger

thefuzzyslug.com
Illustrator *Have Spacesuit, Will Travel*

Corgis make me laugh. The way they sit with their little back legs all splayed to one side, the way they lay all stretched out as far as they can reach with all paws, their big ears, their crooked smiles, and just the way they are a ridiculous delight.

OTHER WORKS: *Thursday's Children; The End of Flesh*

Lisa Mundorff

lisamundorff.com
Illustrator *Will and the Piper*

Growing up as an Oregonian, one of my favorite summertime activities was (and still is) packing a cooler of snacks and heading to a nearby river for the day. We'd bring along some friends and splash around in the Sandy, Clackamas, Willamette, or Estacada Rivers, throwing rocks, digging holes, making dams, and exploring.

OTHER WORKS: *The Small Blue Whale; Friendship Tale (forthcoming)*

Wendy Myers

wendymyersart.com
Illustrator *George Fletcher: The People's Champion*

I have gone swimming on horseback (so technically I was not really swimming, but clinging on) in the Chesapeake Bay. It is really strange and really fun to swim on a horse.

Gina Ochsner

ginaochsner.com
Author *Old as Clouds, Wise as Wind*

I do all my best writing when I'm wearing my Dr. Seuss Cat in the Hat pajamas. It's a body suit/onesie with a long zipper up the front. Thing One with its bright blue hair sits on top of my left foot. Thing Two is on my right. When I wear the pajamas I feel like the world is full of possibility and that anything — anything at all — could and will happen.

OTHER WORKS: *People I Wanted to Be; The Russian Dreambook of Color and Flight; The Hidden Letters of Velta B.*

Brian Parker

believeinwonder.com
Illustrator *A Bucket Full of Dreams*

I grew up in Alaska, and my favorite toy when I was a kid was a stick. A stick could be anything; a sword for slaying monsters, a magic staff for casting spells, or just a simple travelers walking stick.

OTHER WORKS: *Crow in the Hollow; You Can Rely on Platypi; Bennie the Bear*

Valarie Pearce

imarapublishing.com

Author *A Bucket Full of Dreams*

My favorite part of Oregon is Portland. I love the food carts, the bridges, the bike trails, the streets, and the people in the community. My absolute most favorite place in the city is Martin Luther King Jr. Boulevard named after our American hero. Just outside the Oregon Convention Center is an eight-foot bronze statue of Dr. King that I can wave at and remember him every time I pass by.

OTHER WORKS: *When Mommy Needs a Time-Out; When Daddy Needs a Time-Out; I Love Colors*

Dawn Babb Prochovnic

dawnprochovnic.com

Author *First Day Jitters*

I have received only one trophy in my entire life: A Pleasure Reading Award, earned for reading the most books in Mr. Snook's 5th grade class.

OTHER WORKS: *Four Seasons! Five Senses!; The Nest Where I Like to Rest; See the Colors*

Doug Roy

dougroyillustration.com

Illustrator *The Legend of the Mountains' Quarrel*

If I could have any superpower, I would like to have the power to make people happy.

OTHER WORKS: *Pirate Traps; The Emperor's New Clothes; The Van*

Elizabeth Rusch

elizabethrusch.com

Author *Diary of a Volcano*

I once hiked to the top of Mount St. Helens while it was erupting. I could smell the rotten-egg stink of volcanic gas and hear rocks rumbling as new lava pushed old lava rocks out of the way. You could say I'm a little volcano-obsessed. I've written three kids' books about them!

OTHER WORKS: *A Day with No Crayons; For the Love of Music: The Remarkable Story of Maria Anna Mozart; Electrical Wizard: How Nikola Tesla Lit Up the World*

Linda Dalal Sawaya

lindasawaya.com

Illustrator *Meshmesh on Wheels*

I love the Oregon coast because I am a water lover, and my little doggie named Baba Ghannouj, which means "spoiled daddy" in Arabic, loves the beach, too. We love hiking up to the top of Neahkahnie Mountain to watch eagles soar and sit on the rocks, taking in the view and feeling grateful that we made it to the top!

OTHER WORKS: *How to Get Famous in Brooklyn; The Little Ant/La Hormiga Chiquita; Alice's Kitchen: Traditional Lebanese Cooking*

Heidi Schulz

heidischulzbooks.com

Author *The Day the Puddles Stomped Back*

I trick-or-treated my entire childhood. Truly. I didn't stop until long after I became a legal adult. See, I'm not very tall and with a sheet thrown over my head no one could tell I wasn't a child ghost. My favorite kind of Halloween candy is any kind I get trick-or-treating. Except candy corn. That stuff is gross.

OTHER WORKS: *Hook's Revenge; Hook's Revenge: The Pirate Code; Giraffes Ruin Everything*

Stephanie Shaw

stephanieshawauthor.com
Author *Lionel and Pip*

Words make me laugh. Like the word "persnickety." Being "persnickety" isn't particularly funny, but saying it or hearing it, I just may collapse into giggles. Other words that are laugh-producing: galoshes, conundrum, and waggle. You don't think so? Oh, don't be so persnickety.

OTHER WORKS: *A Cookie for Santa; The Legend of the Beaver's Tail; Schnitzel: A Cautionary Tale for Lazy Louts*

Cathy Stever

cathystever.com
Illustrator *Something Fishy*

My favorite books when I was growing up were Nancy Drew mysteries. I love mystery, secret gardens, intrigue, and solving problems. I always tried to guess the ending. Sometimes I guessed right.

OTHER WORKS: *Davenport Cabinet's Our Machine; Jasper's Shadow (forthcoming); Dragon's Chocolate (forthcoming)*

Sonja Thomas

www.bysonjathomas.com
Author *Kira's Imagineering*

I've done the flying trapeze.

OTHER WORKS: A story in *Dark Heart Volume 2;* A story in *2015 Young Explorer's Adventure Guide*

Katy Towell

skarykids.com
Illustrator *Dear Bigfoot*

I love the historic cemetery in Jacksonville, Oregon, because there's SO much history and so much to discover! Even the shapes of some of the headstones have specific meanings and stories. There's even a free coloring and activity book you can grab from the visitor's center.

OTHER WORKS: *Skary Childrin and the Carousel of Sorrow; Charlie and the Grandmothers*

Zoey Abbott Wagner

www.zoeyink.com
Illustrator *Serafina's Tree*

As a kid, I loved the book *The Great Escape: Or, the Sewer Story* by Peter Lippman. I read it until it just about fell apart (but I still have it). This book has it all: great characters, colorful heroes, bad guys, and a triumphant underdog species — alligators.

Johanna Wright

johannawright.com
Illustrator *Moon Song*

I really love what I do, but if I HAD to do something else, I'd probably be a deep-sea diver. I'm actually part mermaid, so this seems like it would be a good fit.

OTHER WORKS: *The Secret Circus; Bunnies on Ice; The Orchestra Pit*

Acknowledgments

To our **Contributing Authors and Illustrators,** thank you for sharing your abilities and creativity with SMART for this project. We are awed by your skill and are fortunate to have each one of you represented in *Oregon Reads Aloud!*

To our fabulous editor, **Michelle McCann,** for the generous donation of her time and expertise — with a heaping side of fun and positivity.

To our *Oregon Reads Aloud* champion and author extraordinaire, **Elizabeth Rusch,** for her vision, passion, and dedication to this project.

To **Melissa Delzio,** our talented designer and founder of the inspiration for our project, *Our Portland Story.*

To **Graphic Arts Books,** an Oregon-based publishing company that loved our project so much they offered to be our publisher. Thank you!

To our **Sponsors,** Arlene Schnitzer, NW Natural, Powell's Books, Regence, The Oregon Community Foundation, The Standard, and Wieden+Kennedy have provided the funding to make this project possible. Thank you for your commitment to empowering kids for reading and learning success.

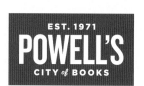

Arlene
Schnitzer

To our *Students:* You're what it's all about. We believe in you, and in the limitless potential that resides within your heads and hearts. Keep reading, keep learning!

To our *Volunteers:* You inspire us each and every day. Your dedication is unmatched, and we are ever grateful for your gift of one of the most precious resources: your time. Over the past 25 years, our volunteers have collectively donated the equivalent of $70 million in time spent reading with Oregon kids. What a tremendous investment in the lives of our children, and in the vitality of our state. Thank you!

To our *Donors:* Your donations are one of the most critical ingredients to our success and the reason we're celebrating 25 years. SMART's work is funded primarily by private sources — individuals, businesses, and foundations — who provide the vital resources needed to fulfill our mission. Thank you for your generosity!

To our *Founders:* Thank you for your vision, your perseverance, your creativity, and your resolve in engaging the community to support Oregon kids, families, and schools in inspiring a love of reading.

To our *Team:* The SMART staff team is one incredible group of folks, each one caring genuinely and passionately about bringing the love of books and reading to local kids. Thank you for all you do. We love you, SMARTies!

To our *Partners:* SMART is far from alone when it comes to the time, resources, access, and infrastructure needed to make the program happen. To our fellow nonprofit organizations, our schools and educators, our supporters — we salute you. Thank you for your support.

Volunteer. Connect. Donate.

We are always in need of volunteers and supporters to help us achieve our mission. To learn more about SMART® and sign up to volunteer, please connect with us.

www.getSMARToregon.org

877.598.4633

 startmakingareadertoday   @getsmartoregon

Oregon
READS
Aloud